FILE UNDER: DECEASED

FILE UNDER: DECEASED

Sarah Lacey

St. Martin's Press
New York

Library of Congress Cataloging-in-Publication Data

Lacey, Sarah.
    File under—deceased / Sarah Lacey.
        p.   cm.
    "A Thomas Dunne book."
    ISBN 0-312-09807-3
    1. Government investigators—England—Fiction.
    2. Women detectives—England—Fiction.   I. Title.
    PR6062.A29F55   1993
    823'.814—dc10   93-25498
                                                              CIP

First published in Great Britain by Hodder and Stoughton Ltd.

First U.S. Edition: September 1993

10 9 8 7 6 5 4 3 2 1

To Trudy
and bilberry pies

CHAPTER ONE

I'VE BEEN TOLD to write down exactly what happened, starting with the day I found myself holding onto a dead man and ending . . . well, there's a lot of ground to cover before I need to think about that, so I'd better begin with basics. My name is Leah Hunter, I'm twenty-five, brown hair, brown eyes, and single from choice; but don't run away with the idea that I hate men, because I don't, men are all right – in their place. I was born and still live in Yorkshire, where puddings and cricket have about equal status. Occasionally one surpasses the other.

I'd taken a long weekend, Friday through Monday, and all I wanted to do was relax and enjoy myself. The first three days had gone according to plan, but Monday fell apart with the weather. When I skipped out there wasn't a cloud in sight, but around lunch-time black billows sailed in like an aerial armada. Around two when the storm finally broke, I took the sensible option and headed for shelter, although as things turned out it would have been more sensible to get a soaking and head for home. I didn't know that then, any more than I knew that when the rain stopped I'd be kneeling in the wet gravel, watching a man die with his head in my lap.

The corpse I found myself cuddling had looked healthy as well as hunky fifteen minutes before. A Tom Cruise look-alike except he had blond hair.

He'd loaned me his catalogue because I'd been too mean to buy one myself. Not that I thought I needed it when the only reason for my being in the damned art gallery was to get out of the rain. If I'd known he was about to meet his Maker I wouldn't have got chatty. My mother has premonitions; I wish the ability was genetic.

1

When big thunder-drops began to hit the windows a small crowd rushed in and stood around in little knots. One was a Chinaman with a grey business suit and neatly furled umbrella. I remember thinking that since the umbrella would have kept him dry he must be the only one who really wanted to see the paintings.

When the rain stopped he followed us outside. He was there watching when my companion folded up like a puppet, and because he was the nearest he was the one I yelled at to get an ambulance.

He smiled politely and walked away.

Someone else went back inside the building and eventually an ambulance came. I watched the two-man crew try to work magic and bring a dead man back to life, but I knew all along it wouldn't work. The thought that he was too young to drop dead like that worried at the back of my mind. Finally they gave up trying and loaded him inside. As the blue flashing light receded, the sun split through a black cloud and drew rainbows in an oily puddle where the ambulance had stood a minute before.

There was no real need for hurry, but as it turned the corner of Dowager Street and joined the main road a sharp flare of sound came from it. I supposed they just liked to play with the siren since a few minutes here or there would make no difference.

Nearby a police car still flashed its blue light at the kerb, and a group of people bunched uneasily near the Art Gallery gates talking to a WPC. The police driver was asking me something, and because concentration wasn't easy at that point the question didn't register. He repeated it.

'I said, I need names and addresses. Yours and your companion's.'

'Leah Hunter, 17a, Palmer's Run, and I don't have a companion.'

His ballpoint stabbed the air in the direction the ambulance had gone. 'You were with him, weren't you?'

'I just happened to be in the wrong place at the wrong time. For me, that is.' I looked him in the eyes, they were

2

grey and knowledgeable, and I knew they didn't always believe what they saw. 'We got talking,' I said, 'that's all. His name was John Thorne, and I don't know where he lived.'

'Your occupation?'

'Tax inspector.'

He looked surprised, but then, most men do. I said, 'Look, we just went round the exhibition room together. When the rain stopped we came outside and he keeled over. I thought it was a faint. Or a fit. Then I realised he was dead.'

'Of course,' he agreed politely. 'Did you try resuscitation before the ambulance came?'

I hadn't and I was feeling guilty about that. It must have shown. Letting me off the hook, he said kindly, 'It probably wouldn't have been any use.'

'No, it wouldn't.' I remembered the blood-stained froth that had spilled over Thorne's chin. 'Dead is dead.' He blinked at that.

The policewoman was filling her notebook with names and addresses, and the group over by the gates was getting smaller. But there had been only one person close enough to see what really happened and he wasn't among them.

I said, 'They missed the main event; the man who saw it all walked away.' He wrote down the description I gave him, which wasn't very good, it would have fitted any Chinaman in a grey suit, but I hadn't been concentrating.

The PC said, 'Are you sure he was Chinese and not Japanese?' I thought about it.

'Malaysian or Vietnamese maybe, but Japanese no, the eyes are different.'

He got back in the car and picked up the radio mike. I turned away. 'Hey!' He got out again. 'You can't go yet.'

A suspicious mind is a terrible thing to have. I pointed to the public bench outside the gallery gates, endowed by the grateful widow of Thomas W. Shepperton. I'd speculated in the past on the reason for her gratitude. 'I'm going to sit down,' I said.

3

The seat was damp but I didn't think it mattered, a grubby patch on my behind would match up nicely with the ones got from kneeling. A single blond hair clung to the denim over my left thigh and I picked it off; it was from Thorne's head. I remembered reading that arsenic poisoning can be detected from a single hair.

Arms spread along the back of the seat, I watched the PC talking urgently into his radio. I felt in sympathy with him. He had an unexplained death on his hands and for all he knew it could be murder.

The idle, unwanted thought expanded. Who would be the chief suspect? Who had been with the dead man at the time? The policewoman's eyes met mine, and I knew I could find myself answering a lot of questions.

Imagination is a good thing to have but sometimes mine conjured up things that were just too way over the top, and this was one of them.

John Thorne had probably eaten too many chips, too many cream buns and although I hadn't seen him do it, probably smoked like a chimney and earned a heart attack. A plain, simple heart attack. No mystery about that.

The police officers consulted, their eyes fixed on me. They came over with pussy-cat smiles, sure I wouldn't mind being driven to the police station.

I didn't share their expectations.

'For why? I didn't even know the man.' They decided to try charm before the handcuffs came out.

'Just routine form-filling, that kind of thing. You won't be kept long.' The words were smooth but my mind pounced on the word 'kept' and worried at it. I didn't see why I should be kept at all.

I voiced my feelings.

The answer came back as though the velvet glove was wearing thin. One word. 'Procedure.' The three of us trooped back to the car.

As we sat side by side the policewoman tried the pussy-cat grin again. 'You'll find it painless, questions aren't anything to worry about, you'll be home in no time.'

The words I knew were meant to be reassuring but

4

they failed miserably. My dentist promised painless meetings too.

Then I realised there could be a bright side to things, like a ready-made excuse to miss my elder, seriously married sister's dinner invitation. It wasn't the meal itself I objected to, it was the 'extra' man she would have dug up from somewhere. She and I have vastly different tastes.

I said generously, 'It really doesn't matter that much, I'm in no hurry, take whatever time it needs,' and leaned back comfortably.

It was then that the memory of Thorne's face came back to mind, the startled look as his knees buckled. When I knelt and lifted his head from the wet, gritty path there had been pain and panic in his eyes, and I didn't want to remember it.

I sat upright and stared at the passing buildings. He'd been past speech, fighting for breath, and his eyes had rolled and met mine, full of death. Balanced on the brink of the abyss I'd had to watch him fall in.

I wished I could wash the image from my mind.

According to family lore great-grandmother had a glimpse of heaven as she died, and stepped across the threshold singing hallelujah. It had probably held the nice comfortable things that she had anticipated since childhood.

Thorne's eyes hadn't seen the same visions, of that I was sure.

Unexpectedly perceptive the WPC said, 'It's like that sometimes. The shock hits you hard when you don't expect it.'

'It isn't shock,' I said. 'I just remembered the way he looked when he died.'

'That's shock. First you forget, then you remember. Is there anything new I should know about?'

'Nothing that would help. Just the look in his eyes. It must have been his heart, I mean healthy people don't drop dead, do they?'

'Not unless they have a little help.'

I looked at the bland face suspiciously as the car stopped. 'From whom?'

She didn't tell me, instead, she said, 'The canteen tea isn't that bad and you look as if you need a cup.' Then she got out and waited for me. 'Where did he live?' she added casually.

'No idea. I told you; I didn't know him. But it would have been a nice try,' I conceded, 'if I had.'

I was at the police station an hour; time flies when you're having a good time. The detective sergeant who came to talk to me was interesting, and interested too from the way he looked me over. I returned the appraisal, starting at the top and working my way down, lingering a little, as he had, before coming back up again. He pretended not to notice but the dimple at the side of his mouth gave him away. It was a nice mouth. I wondered why Em couldn't find someone like him to ask to dinner.

Then I remembered what had happened to the last man I found interesting. I hoped Detective Sergeant Nicholls was in a better state of health.

He thanked me nicely when it came to leaving time and said they wouldn't be wanting to interview me again, which was oddly disappointing. I smiled at him encouragingly and he smiled back, closed his file of papers and went away.

I walked home slowly and called in at a late opening mini-mart two streets away. When I finally let myself into the attic flat, it was late enough to ring Em and tell her with complete honesty that I couldn't possibly drive the thirty miles to Ledford in time for dinner.

I knew she'd complain about it, and she did. She had this perfectly darling man lined up for me, who was a whizz in computers. Knowing Em, he was probably part of the keyboard. I'd heard Em's promises before.

It was a shame the barrel she continually scraped never showed signs of yielding someone like the detective sergeant. I said goodbye and hung up remembering the last 'really nice man' she had found for me.

He'd been into some kind of shifty finance operation and I hadn't liked his chunky gold bracelet, or the hair that was just a mite too long for forty plus.

When the stock question came up: 'And what do *you* do with yourself all day?' I'd batted the eyelashes triple mascaraed for Em's benefit, before I gave it to him straight.

'I track down tax evaders,' I told him sweetly.

Em hadn't been pleased, I was always a disappointment to her, and I wondered why she didn't give up.

I took a shower, cooked the stir-fry from the mini-mart, and went to bed with a book. Later in the night I dreamed of John Thorne. We were back on the path in the rain, and his head was in my lap. This time his eyes were dead and his mouth alive, red froth spun out of it like sugar candy and spelled out words I couldn't read. The Chinaman gathered them into his umbrella and walked away. One drifted back like a piece of red lace and settled on the catalogue I held in my hand, this time I could read it, it said, *Murder.*

CHAPTER TWO

PETE INNES CAME over to my desk. He has an odd way of walking, leaning forward slightly as if he were a dancing master. Not mincing exactly, but very near. He asked if I'd had an amusing day off, and dumped a bulky file in front of me before I could tell him.

'There's a query from the cop shop, love, they'd like a bit of inside information.'

As usual his hand was a bony pink spider on my shoulder and he'd been at the peppermints again. The minty scent wafted from his breath and I fought an urge to swat at the fingers.

'Thirty-five and dropped dead.' He shuddered and the fingers twitched. 'I worry sometimes.'

Anyone seeing the red vein motorways in his eyes knew he had need to. He made me an offer. 'Better grab me while you can, Leah love, who knows how long I'll be around?'

'Only the good die young, Pete, you're safe.'

That pleased him and he patted my hand and moved away.

Looking at the tax file he'd left behind gave me a sense of *déjà vu*. The name on it was *John Thorne* and someone had stamped across it *Deceased*.

For some reason I got an aggrieved feeling on Thorne's behalf. Tax files like bank accounts are private, or should be, but dying changes all that, the dead can't complain about civil liberties.

I wondered why Pete had decided to dump it on me when normally I only deal with oddities, then I opened it up and found that Thorne could come into that category, he'd moved around the country like a demented rabbit.

A few months here, a few months there and not always, I noted, doing the same job.

Teacher, reporter, salesman, photographer, and – I looked again – a bouncer at a strip club. When he died he'd been working as a security guard.

I noted all these comings and goings for police interest; I noted too that he didn't owe HM Government anything. I was glad he'd gone with a clear conscience.

I began to wonder why the police were interested in his affairs. Not simply because it had been a sudden death or we'd have a steady flow of requests through the office. People were always meeting Nemesis in unexpected places.

I let imagination play around with the idea of spy and counter-spy, but both of them were out of fashion since *glasnost* and *perestroika* changed the world view. Still . . . there was that Chinaman . . .

I had the file extracts for the police typed up and delivered by hand, hoping that would be the end of it. I was quite ready to forget all about Thorne, but mid-afternoon the office copy of the evening paper arrived with two column inches devoted to his death. The last line hit me like an ice-cube.

Police are treating the death as suspicious.

I didn't want to know that; I wanted it to have been a plain, natural demise. Damn it, I'd been with him, what did they mean – suspicious? I flipped over to the courts page and concentrated on all those things people get up to and don't want the tax office to know about. Reading about the scams they were into was less worrying than thinking about Thorne.

Bramfield isn't all that big a place, in fact if you compare the dot that represents it on a map with the splash that's given to Manchester, it looks as if a fly has lifted its leg in passing. But then again it isn't all that small. The main street is about a mile long and bends in the middle to form a clumsy L. Traffic from the south runs straight on to it, and surprise surprise, traffic coming out the other end finds itself funnelled onto the ring-road and going back the same way, like in an Escher drawing.

9

The largest shops and half a dozen chainstores are grouped along it, and there's a fancy new shopping centre in the bend of the L.

There are also fourteen nite-spots, wine bars, and disco bars, and dotted between them ten pubs. Which is why the police presence on Saturday nights is awe-inspiring.

When I left the office I didn't go straight home. Tuesdays and Thursdays I go to the Health Club and spend some time on the Nautilus machines they installed last year. They're very flash and American looking, and even a seven-stone weakling can feel good hooked up to all that chrome and leather.

That's something else Em and I don't see eye to eye on. She doesn't believe women need biceps or self-defence classes; not when there are big strong men around to look after them.

I didn't like to remind her about the thirty-four reported rapes, committed by those same big strong Bramfield men over the past twelve months. Em has always been naive about such things, which is why she still played in Wendy Houses when I was learning to arm wrestle.

It was nearly eight when I got home, and the first thing I noticed was a Telecom van parked on the street. I'd been expecting a repair man to call and tell me why the telephone allowed calls out and not in, but I hadn't expected overtime. I'd given Marcie on the middle floor a key, and on my way up I called in to ask how long they'd been there.

She said, 'Hi, Leah,' and gave me back the key.

I looked at it and said stupidly, 'They've gone?'

'Hours since. Three o'clockish.' She stuck her head on one side, hauling her two-year-old up on one hip. 'Why? Something the matter?'

'No. No, everything's fine. Thanks, Marcie.'

'Any time.'

I went on upstairs. I'd left a note stuck on the door with Sellotape. 'Telecom. Key below at flat two.' It was gone now. I turned the key and walked into what had once been a tidy hideaway and was now a mess. Everything was on

10

the floor, the drawers had been emptied, the cupboards too. A look in the bedroom and kitchen showed the same chaos. It never rains but what it pours.

I found the telephone buried under a pile of belongings and dialled 999, surprised it was working, then I went to sit on the top stair until the police came.

When they did it was with a flashy scream of brakes that carried up to the third floor. I wondered if they'd been taking corners on two wheels, a sort of Dirty Harry come to Yorkshire, and fantasised on that until they came into view. Clint Eastwood they were not.

Both were in uniform, one around minimum height and the other maximum weight. I sighed and got up. They stood in the doorway and surveyed the mess.

'Go on in,' I invited. 'Make yourselves at home – the burglar did.'

Laurel took out his notebook and Hardy raised his eyebrows.

'It's a mess. A thorough job.' He made it sound as if he felt he should give an efficiency award. I champed my bottom lip and he seemed to think it was to stop from crying. It wasn't, of course, I was damn angry at the cleaning up I'd have to do and didn't want to take it out on them. He patted my shoulder anyway.

'We'll sort it out.'

'Thank you,' I said, 'PC 158.'

'Renshaw,' he corrected, 'and he's PC Clift.'

Clift said, 'What's gone then?' and poised his biro.

I said, 'I don't know,' and felt stupid. He sighed.

'Can you have a look round, love.'

I looked. After a while I came back to them. 'Nothing,' I said.

They looked at each other. Clift said, 'Well, if nothing's missing, it must be somebody doesn't like you, love.'

Renshaw moved off and poked around while I thought about that. He came back and examined the door lock.

'Who else has got a key then?' he asked.

'No one.'

'Can't see any signs of a break-in.'

11

'Probably the Telecom man didn't lock the door when he left. I gave Marcie downstairs a key so he could get in.'

'And he's been?'

'About three, according to Marcie.' I remembered something. 'Which is odd because he seems to have gone off and left his van behind. It's still parked up the street.'

They looked at each other and clattered off without comment. Naturally I followed.

The telephone engineer hadn't left his van at all, he was still in it, wearing blue jockeys with red spots and a white T-shirt. Someone had tied his hands to his ankles and stuffed a handkerchief in his mouth. The logo on his shirt was apt, it said, 'A Tetley's Bitter Man' and he looked it.

Clift climbed in the back and untied him. He said kindly, 'You all right, mate?'

The Telecom man said, 'I could do with a leak.'

I left them to it and went to put the kettle on. After a bit Renshaw came upstairs and saw me cramming things back into cupboards.

'Don't do that, love, if you don't mind, we've got CID coming, they'll want to see it as it is. Not a simple break-in now, is it? Assault is a serious matter.'

'You mean you might try to catch someone?' I said politely, and he gave me a funny look. 'I've made some tea if you want a cup. What about the other two?'

'On their way to hospital.' He confided. 'Telecom engineer got a clout over the head. I'd be interested to know what you've got up here to make it worth all that trouble to get in.'

'So would I,' I assured him. 'So would I.'

I made us both a sandwich and we ate amicably until the door bell rang. I let Renshaw go to open it and picked the kettle up again; there seemed to be a lot of voices. When I heard a pair of feet come into the kitchen I turned the tap off and asked.

'Is it CID?'

A voice that was not Renshaw's said mildly, 'You didn't have to go to all this trouble to get to see me again.' I turned and found Detective Sergeant Nicholls

12

standing in the doorway and decided things were looking up.

I'd been right about there being a lot of voices. Suddenly my poor ransacked flat merited a fingerprint crew and a photographer.

'So what happened exactly?' Nicholls said.

I poured him a cup of tea and found an untrodden packet of chocolate biscuits. A firm believer in making the best of things, that's me.

I sat down opposite him. 'You tell me,' I said. 'All I wanted was the telephone repaired.' I munched thoughtfully. 'The door has a five lever lock, so my guess is somebody read the note I left and waited for the Telecom man to come.'

'Which means,' he followed on logically, 'that this somebody thought there was something here worth waiting for. You wouldn't know what that was, I suppose?'

'No.'

It was my flat that had been ransacked and me that would have to do all the tidying up and I was beginning to get angry. Why did I suddenly have the feeling I was being made chief culprit too? I said sarcastically, 'There are art treasures under the floorboards. Why else?'

'Funny you should say that,' he said. 'Which floor boards?'

I stared at him. He was joking of course; turning sarcasm neatly round and winding me up. But he didn't seem to be laughing.

I said, 'For pity's sake, I don't have anything worth stealing except the hi-fi, and he didn't take that.'

'Wouldn't have been worth the effort expended,' he answered insultingly. 'You're sure nothing is missing?'

'I haven't checked the spoons yet.'

He looked at that sticking out of the sugar basin and grinned. Then he said, 'Thanks for the information you sent round this afternoon. It was your signature, wasn't it?'

'On the tax extracts, yes. What did you need them for?'

13

Instead of answering he tossed another question. 'Thorne didn't give you anything, did he? When you were in the gallery or outside on the path?'

'I thought we'd been through that,' I said plaintively. 'No, he didn't give me anything.' I folded my arms and felt aggrieved.

Then the penny dropped. If DS Nicholls thought I had something belonging to Thorne, ergo he thought something belonging to Thorne was what my burglar had been searching for.

I said, 'There's something about Thorne I don't know, isn't there? Something that isn't in our files. Why are you so interested in him?'

He shifted uneasily and got up. 'I'd better see how they're doing,' he said and took himself into the living room. A man with a puffer brush and a roll of Sellotape took his place.

'Don't mind me,' he said cheerfully getting to work on a cupboard door. 'Put your feet up and relax if you feel like it.'

'Thanks,' I said. 'It's really nice to know I can make myself at home.'

Before he left, Nicholls came in and ate the last chocolate biscuit. 'I fixed the phone,' he said kindly. 'It was just a loose connection.'

'There's a lot of them around,' I agreed darkly, and put the kettle on again.

CHAPTER THREE

MARCIE CAME TO help me clean up. She was suffering from a guilt complex. A lot of things had got broken, including a pottery cat that had lived docilely on a low table. It wasn't worth anything, just a bit of nineteen-sixtyish kitsch found on a market stall, but I'd grown attached to it and now it was a jigsaw puzzle. She helped me put the bits in a bin liner, twittering all the time about how stupid she'd been and how she ought to have stayed there with the Telecom man.

I said briskly, 'To begin with he wasn't one, and body bags are shiny black plastic too.' That shut her up. She sat back on her heels and looked at me while it sank in.

'He was just a sneak thief.'

'Uh-huh. Sneak thieves take things, this one just wrecked the place. If you'd been around . . .'

She stuck both index fingers in her ears. 'Don't tell me,' she begged.

By the time we'd finished, the plastic sack was about full, but I didn't take it out to the dustbins until the next morning; for some reason I didn't want to go out to the backyard in the dark. Which was lucky, because if I hadn't waited for daylight, I wouldn't have seen the catalogue on top of the previous day's rubbish.

It wasn't mine – it had been John Thorne's, I'd been going to give it back to him as we came out of the exhibition.

I'd had it in my hand, holding it out, when he fell over, and then I guess I must have pushed it into my jeans pocket, because when I dumped them in the washer it had fallen out and I'd dropped it in the waste basket without thinking. I

15

remembered how many times I'd told the police he hadn't given me anything.

I brushed wet tea-leaves off the cover and took it back upstairs. A lacy red tomato stain sat in one corner, and I looked at it uneasily, I don't like to be reminded of nightmares. It was only a local art exhibition, for God's sake, and the amateurish catalogue had been designed on somebody's computer and then photo-copied. Most of it was taken up with adverts for places like 'Jack's Chippy', or 'Mildred's Hats For Those More Formal Occasions'. I'd seen some of those hats. Mrs Shilling would have died laughing.

Skipping through it while I ate breakfast made me feel slightly ridiculous. Absurd to think this was why someone had turned my flat inside out.

Imagination stirred. Micro-dots and coded messages; a whole spy network centred round an art exhibition. George Smiley telling me I'd saved England.

I rinsed the pots and went to work, the catalogue crammed into my handbag. If I had time, or remembered, I'd pass it on to DS Nicholls.

Because things often crop up that make me work on after the five o'clock sigh of relief, I usually have a backlog of time I can either take back or get paid for. I try to split it fifty-fifty, that way I sometimes get a nice little bonus and still have enough time owing to take a day off if I feel like it. At three that afternoon I was scheduled for a long, and probably vexing, tax argument with a market trader named Ron. It's an amicable running battle, as soon as I plug up one tax leak he thinks up a new scam. Up to now he hasn't managed to get ahead, but the extra hour I took mid-day was to fortify me. I sympathised with Ron; if I were on the other side of my desk I'd try to get out of paying taxes too.

The thundery spell had gone and the weather was cooler now, but still sunny and hot enough to fill up meagre grassy patches with sun-bathers. Walking up the gravel drive to the art gallery, over the spot where Thorne had died, gave me a funny feeling, but I wanted to take another, and longer look inside. So far the only thing I'd come up with that made the catalogue in my handbag different to any of its fellows, was a ring around the numbers of two paintings. I vaguely remembered one of them for its awfulness.

The artist had given away the entire range of his imaginative skills in its title: *Autumn Woods on a Wet Day*.

This time, in a flush of generosity, I supported local arts and bought a catalogue of my own. The woman seated in the foyer behind a leggy formica table looked grateful; except on wet days Bramfielders aren't exactly culture hounds. I didn't envy her. The dado extending nearly halfway up the walls was gingery brown, and the wall above had been emulsioned a slightly paler shade of mustard than the carpet tiles on the floor. Just passing through made me nauseous.

Standing in front of painting number 135 confirmed first impressions, and I couldn't think why anyone would like it enough to pay good money for it – but someone had, a red sticker on the top right-hand corner of the frame said so. The other painting Thorne picked out had been sold too. I peered at the name written in tiny letters. Someone called Pickles had a split personality. *Blue Nude with Carnation* didn't go with a wet day in the woods. Or perhaps Mr Pickles knew more about art than I did and was set to make a killing.

It was a bad choice of words and I moved away to look at a seascape. Casually I ringed its number in the catalogue I'd bought, then did the same for the Grandma Moses type painting of a fair that was flat, and out of perspective, but quite jolly. Neither of them had earned a red sticker.

I put the pen back in my handbag and touched an ancient tube of fruit gums in the bottom; on the way out I offered one to the lonely woman in the foyer, and she took it and scrutinised it carefully before shrugging and putting it in her mouth.

She said, 'You were here Monday, weren't you, when it rained and, er, um . . .?' I finished it for her.

'When the man dropped dead outside.'

17

'I thought I'd got it right,' she said. 'Must have been upsetting.' I agreed that it had been. 'I'd have come to help,' she added defensively, 'but I'm not allowed to leave the paintings.'

'Of course not,' I murmured. 'Who knows what thieves may be about?' Which was rather prescient of me considering that when I got outside one of them gave me a violent push and grabbed at my bag. The catalogue I'd been trying to cram inside dropped to the ground as we played pull devil pull baker.

The thought passed through my mind that self-defence classes should have taught me more than this. I admired the fishnet stocking over his face and thought about screaming. I also wondered how long the Marks and Spencer bag would stand the strain. He must have had the same thought because he let go with one hand and reached into his pocket.

I remembered the counter-move to that.

The pirouette was neat, my instructor would have been proud. When I kicked his knee-cap and his leg gave way, the heel of my shoe was in the right place to meet something soft and satisfyingly crunchy.

I wished I could scream like that, if I had he would probably have run away in the first place.

Bag clasped like a baby I backed away and found the street frozen like a film still. There was a bus at the stop by the gates, and as I got on I saw the bag snatcher's hand reach for the catalogue I'd let fall. I didn't go back for it, he deserved a consolation prize.

I should have called in at the police station and reported it, I know that, but if I had I would have been tied up for the greater part of the afternoon and I had an appointment to keep. The way things turned out it didn't really matter because they got to know anyway.

As the bus had pulled away from the stop I'd seen the woman from the exhibition take a quick look out of the door. When she saw the fishnet stocking she'd slammed it shut, and I had a feeling the gallery had closed for the day.

18

They say any publicity is better than no publicity; if the exhibition kept on like this it would be a sell-out.

Safe behind locked doors she had obviously dialled 999, because when I came out of the interview room and shook hands amicably with Ron the artful dodger, DS Nicholls was in the waiting area with his feet up on a low table.

He said, 'You need a minder, has anybody told you that?'

'My sister,' I said shortly and he looked surprised. It wasn't his fault that he'd hit on a touchy subject, but I didn't intend explaining it either.

He took his feet down and said sternly 'I suppose you weren't going to mention having your handbag snatched.'

I said, 'Yes, I was actually, and it wasn't, I still have it, which should prove I don't need a minder. I would have come in on my way home if you'd given me the chance.'

'There'd have been more hope of catching him if you'd told us at the time. We'd have had a description, for one thing.'

'Easy,' I said grandly. 'He has a fetish for fishnet stockings, a limp, and he's probably just bought himself a new jock strap at Boots.'

He stared down at the carpet. 'Height?'

'Five-ten, five-eleven.'

'What about his voice, Yorkshire, southern, foreign . . .'

'Falsetto.'

He looked at me and his face twitched, then he started laughing. Eventually he stopped and told me to collect my things. Obediently I walked down to the police car with him. Maybe this time he'd tell me what was going on.

CHAPTER FOUR

I MADE ANOTHER statement. This time I knew the ropes, and the tea had a familiar taste to it.

Nicholls said, 'This could be the man who played jumble sale with your flat yesterday, had you thought of that?' He said it in that superior way men have when they don't believe the little woman has a clue about something. I was disappointed.

'If we're exchanging confidences,' I said, 'I had a thought of my own along the lines of none of this would have happened if it hadn't rained on Monday, and that being so it would be nice to know why I'm being picked on. What exactly was Thorne's role in life? An undercover agent? A superspy? A . . .'

'A security guard, you have it on file.'

'For exactly six weeks he was,' I said. 'And I suppose he moved around and changed jobs so often to escape affiliation orders.' I was aggrieved again, if I'd been inflicted with a death, a break-in and a mugging in the space of three days, damn it I deserved to know why. 'Mutual co-operation could be mutually rewarding,' I pointed out. 'If I have to play piggy-in-the-middle I'd like to know who's trying to fry my bacon.'

We stared at each other. I once had a teddy bear with blue eyes and a friendly face. Maybe that was why Nicholls attracted me, although of course there were other things in his favour teddy hadn't possessed.

He sounded suspicious. 'You wouldn't be withholding information?'

'Of course not,' I gave him my ingenue smile. One more lie wouldn't damn my soul. 'How *did* Thorne die?'

'Why not wait for the inquest?'

20

'Because the way things are going life could be too short, if I meet my end in a dark alley you'll regret not telling me.' I didn't, of course, intend to let that happen, but I put a tremble in my voice anyway.

For a minute it looked as if he would reach out and hold my hand, but instead he shuffled his papers around while he thought about what I'd said.

'I wouldn't mind knowing your part in it myself,' he said finally, 'and if and when I find out you'll be the first to know.' There was a ring of truth that hung round his head like a halo, it almost hid the half-threat of handcuffs when he did find out. He picked up the zip-topped handbag from the table and looked at it. His voice was friendly again. 'A beef-sized mugger floored by a pint-sized tax inspector. I wish I'd seen it.'

'He wasn't that big,' I said modestly, and waited to be admired some more, but I was disappointed again, all he did was drop the bag back on the table.

He said, 'Well, whatever you had in here is still safe.'

I picked it up and set it on the floor.

'I wouldn't go that far. I dropped a catalogue, and since he seemed to want to keep it I thought I'd let him.'

'A catalogue.'

'One of those duplicated things for the art exhibition. Thorne gave me his but I threw it away Monday night.'

He sat forward and his eyes lost the teddy-bear look. 'You said he hadn't given you anything.'

'I'd forgotten about it, it was in my hand when he folded up, I must have pushed it in my pocket without thinking. Damn it, they're only twenty pence each, I bought my own today.'

'And which one did you drop?'

'Mine.'

'And the other is where?'

'In the bag.' I fished it out. He looked at it with some criticism. The tea leaves were gone but the stains were still there, and the back was even worse. Dustbins aren't the most hygienic places.

He slid it into a plastic bag. 'Thanks,' he said. 'With any luck you won't be bothered again.'

I wished I could be so certain. If all the aggro had been over a catalogue, the wrong one could make matters worse. The idea floated across my mind that finding out what was going on couldn't be that much harder than keeping track of tax evaders. It was all a matter of knowing the right questions to put to the right people.

I stood up.

Nicholls said, 'There's mug shots to look at, you can't go yet.'

'It's almost seven. Any time now my stomach starts to rumble.'

He had a persuasive smile. I guessed his mother must have taught him he'd catch more flies with a honey pot than a vinegar jar.

'Suppose I offer to feed your stomach and drive you home?'

It sounded something of a bargain. If I discounted McDonalds and the eight fish and chip shops, Bramfield offered Indian, Chinese and Italian cuisine; I decided he would go for Italian but I was wrong, bargains are invariably not what they seem and the police canteen didn't deserve a single star.

The next two days were busy and they were also uneventful. Thorne *et al.* went into the back of my mind.

Saturday mornings I take a gentle jog to the park, do a couple of circuits around the perimeter path, and then jog gently home again. If it's wet and the rain is light I do the same thing, but today it was raining as though it had been saving up for a year. The bouncing drops on the windowsill made me remember the Chinaman and his umbrella.

I made coffee and toast and ate with my feet up while I read the local paper. On the third page there was a photograph of the art gallery with a caption that read: JINXED EXHIBITION CLOSES TODAY, and underneath in smaller letters, THEFT FOLLOWS DEATH AND MUGGING.

Crime was a growth industry. I read the rest, glad that no one had got my name. There wasn't anything I didn't already know about the death and mugging, but the theft was news. Thieves had broken in through a basement window sometime Wednesday night. It didn't specify which paintings had been taken, but I thought I could guess.

I made another guess too: that they'd gone before Detective Sergeant Nicholls had got a look at them. It part made up for the greasy chips and plastic egg.

At eleven, with the rain still teeming, I abandoned any idea of jogging, and substituted a visit to the health club.

I keep a car in a garage at the bottom of the street, the garage is rented from Dora who is pushing seventy and doesn't drive. It's an arrangement that suits both of us very well. She waved at me through her window as I backed down the drive, her hair a hedgehog of rollers. I waved back and the engine misfired and coughed a little more pollution out.

The only thing wrong with working out at the health club is the all-female company. From time to time I make the suggestion that mixed sessions might be fun, but it doesn't have any effect. Tuesdays, Thursdays and Saturday mornings are lady days, and the rest of the week, unless you're on anabolic steroids, it's out of bounds.

I usually avoid Saturdays because the clientele changes. Tuesday and Thursday evenings we're all serious; Saturday morning it's designer day, pale mauve and lemon Lycra fighting it out with tiger prints. I ignored the social sniping and did what I'd come for.

Don't run away with the notion that I'm muscle bound because I'm not. Every time I go home I get mother-grumbles about being too thin. The thing is, I don't want to run out of steam by the time I get to fifty, bodies can't be traded in like cars, so I look after mine.

I followed up with a sauna and a cold shower and got a coffee and sandwich in the coffee shop. On the way home I decided to pay another visit to the gallery.

The same woman was sitting in the foyer, I thought she

was looking a little older but it could have been the bad light. It was still raining a torrent outside and the natural light was dull grey, which didn't mix well with a yellowish glow from the spindly wood chandelier hanging from the ceiling. She looked unhappy when she saw me. Today she had a companion, an elderly gentleman who didn't look as though he'd pose much of a threat to an intruder.

I bought another catalogue and she said, 'I do hope you have a better day.' I hoped so too. When I moved into the big room where the paintings were I saw her watching me warily as she spoke to her companion, then his head swivelled round too. I gave them both what I hoped would be a reassuring smile and moved out of sight.

The paintings, most of them, still looked what they were – amateurish; the colours just that bit too bright, the perspective not exactly right, although one or two deserved better company. But I hadn't come back to admire them, I'd come from the same curiosity that killed the cat. I wanted to know which were missing, having already decided where the gaps would be.

I sat on one of the viewing chairs and looked at the empty spots. Two things were obvious: Mr Pickles, whoever he was, had lost his paintings, and the mugger's prize didn't seem to have caused confusion after all.

CHAPTER FIVE

ON THE WAY out I stopped in the foyer for a chat. Although the woman at the table didn't seem too keen on the idea, she was too polite to say so.

'It's been a pretty bad week,' I said. 'All in all.'

There was something of a hunted look in the woman's eyes. The outer door opened twice and three more viewers passed through the foyer. Her eyes left me and followed them.

'I remember the two stolen paintings had red sale stickers,' I went on. 'Mr Pickles must be disappointed, although I suppose it's equally bad news for the artist, losing two good sales like that.' I hoped I'd struck the right note, I'm not very good at that kind of small talk. Obviously I had because her eyes swivelled back.

'Well, yes, that's right,' she agreed, 'and of course it's the first time that particular artist has shown with us, that's very upsetting. Newcomers to exhibiting tend to have such fragile confidence at the best of times.'

'Mm-mm, that must make it worse,' I sympathised. 'A new member of the art club too?'

'Well – er . . . no, er . . . he isn't actually one of our own members, the summer exhibition has always been open, so anyone can hang if they pay the entrance fee, not like Christmas, when it's just art club members.' She leaned across the table confidentially and I bent forward. 'The disturbing thing is that we got a wrong address for the artist, the police haven't been able to let him know yet.'

'Upsetting.'

'That's right. And we don't know what to do with Mr Pickles' deposit either.'

Another punter wandered in and she sat up straight. I

25

waited. Her companion made a quick catalogue sale and then went into the Gents. I said, 'Does that mean you don't have an address for Mr Pickles?'

She stacked catalogues into a neat pile and then split it into three. Then she stacked them back together, not looking at me now.

'Oh, I shall be so glad when it's all over,' she said in a burst. 'It's made me really nervous, a dreadful week, a really dreadful week, thank heavens it's the last day. I'm surprised you've come back after what's happened already. Do be careful as you go out.'

I would, but I wasn't ready to go yet, there was something else I wanted to know. She shied away when I suggested she could give a good description of both artist and buyer.

'Oh, my dear, I don't know. Ellen was manning the table last week not me, and Jeremy took the entries of course being club secretary, you'd need to ask them.'

The door to the Gents opened and a look of relief came over her face. 'Do take care, dear,' she said, and scurried into the Ladies.

I tried for eye contact with her companion, but he ignored the come-hither and walked on into the exhibition room. I took the hint and went home.

By Sunday morning the rain had passed over but the sky held nothing but mawky grey; I didn't mind that, I didn't even mind the puddles that had been left behind.

I pulled on black sweats and jogging shoes and headed for the park. A lot of the regulars I normally see on Saturday mornings had done the same thing.

It's a funny thing about jogging, you get to know a lot of people for short bursts of time. Somebody comes up, pants along at the side of you for a while, passes the time of day, then hares off. I enjoyed it. Neat, tangle free relationships. I did my two circuits and jogged gently home.

I'd been trying not to think. I tend to do that a lot too. Worrying at a problem doesn't seem to help much and I take the opposite approach: ignore it for long enough and the answer comes up and taps you on the shoulder practically begging for attention.

This morning all the answers seemed to be out of condition, not only had they not caught up with me, I couldn't even hear them panting in the distance.

The pavements had dried off, with only an occasional shy puddle left where broken paving stones dipped and formed a basin, they looked dark and non-reflective under the sulking cloud cover but in one, a little larger than most, two sparrows were skinny dipping. They stopped when I trotted past and I felt like a party pooper, but when I got to the corner and looked round they were back again having fun.

I jogged past nineteen-thirtyish semis and the smell of roast-beef dinners. Half the men seemed to be out washing cars and I mused about yesterday's desirable residences moving down-market. Around the time my mother was born this had been the 'posh' bit of Bramfield, now the flash money had moved out around the lake and drove BMWs big enough to house a Third World family.

I reached the converted Victorian villas of Palmer's Run.

Since the break-in we flat dwellers had decided to keep the front door locked, which I suppose we should have done all along, but you can get lazy about these things. I opened it up and made the long haul upstairs to shower and change before I drove to Scorsby Bridge.

I'd driven there before for pleasure, this time it was mixed with business. It took a while to find a parking spot. Scorsby is a popular place for Sunday trippers, especially in summer, and the market-place was packed with stalls and crowded with shoppers.

Nothing breeds envy like success, and my, how the less successful love to blow the whistle.

Sometimes I think I'm in the wrong job, because I have this sneaking admiration for Ron. I joined the jostling mob around his stall, he had his arms up in the air and a box of chocolates in each hand.

'I don't have to tell you what you'd pay for these down

your local shop, do I, or the supermarket either? Think yourself lucky if you paid a fiver each for 'em, wouldn't you? Well I don't want a fiver each, I don't even want four pounds. Three pounds the two – who'll have 'em?'

A sea of hands rose and he did a brisk trade. I elbowed through and offered him three pounds. He took it without a blink.

'Made my day, you have,' he affirmed loudly to the crowd's delight. 'What a gorgeous bit of skirt this is, gentlemen, don't you think so – well, you'd think so if she didn't 'ave her trousers on, wouldn't you?' There was laughter. A wag at the back shouted, 'Get 'em off.' Ron gave me a wide wink and a smile to go with it. He leaned forward. 'Leave us your address, me old darling, and I'll be round tomorrow.'

'I'll expect it,' I told him, 'make it early,' and elbowed off with my prize. When I looked back he was in full flow again, making the best of things, thin black hair falling forward, fortyish face charming the punters, and a dozen chocolate bars fast changing hands for two pounds.

I backed out of the parking spot and headed home. Ron would be wondering who had been having a quiet word about his Sunday trading activities, undeclared for tax purposes.

When I got back to Bramfield the one-way road system took me past the house where Thorne had lived, and I pulled up outside. When I'd seen the address in his tax file I'd been surprised; the address didn't fit in with the brief impression I'd had of him. The people who lived along here would never give me worries; only the landlords earned enough to pay taxes. The house where Thorne had roomed was part of an Edwardian terrace, all red brick and sash windows with mean little front gardens boasting a bit of grass and not much else. There was a card in the bottom window that read 'Room to Let'.

Across the street another terrace stared depressingly back, and I knew Thorne hadn't chosen to live here for the view. Maybe he'd just wanted to go to ground.

A net curtain moved in the downstairs window as

28

whoever stood behind it returned my interest. I got out and locked up. Against the camber of the road my elderly Mini looked like it had been hitting the bottle. I patted it gently and went to ring the bell.

There were four stone steps so steep that when the sun-cracked door opened I was nose level with beer-gut. An outsize and greyish T-shirt didn't quite make it over the bulge. I gave the droopy, unshaven face a forgiving smile, but he didn't appreciate it.

'It's let,' he said and closed the door. Charming! I really like rude people, they make it so easy to be nasty. I kept a finger on the bell and he came back. This time I didn't smile.

'Tax officer.' I flashed my ID. 'Is this your property?'

'What if it is?'

'How many rooms and how much rent? And a list of tenants. Won't take long, I'll come in, shall I?' I set a foot on the top step and he fell back unwillingly.

'It's Sunday,' he complained belligerently. 'Not bleedin' office hours, is it?' Thumbs in belt he hoisted and the gap momentarily closed.

'Horses for courses,' I told him obliquely. 'What about a recent tax statement, that might help, and I don't suppose you live solely on the rents; you'll be paying PAYE from another job?' He looked shifty and I made a wild guess. 'I take it this is a registered property complying with fire regulations and public health?'

He said, 'I got four tenants and five rooms; two sharing top back, two singles in front. Twenty each double, twenty-four single.'

'You won't mind showing me round then,' I said. 'Just for the records.'

He minded, it showed in his bullish eyes. I felt glad his IQ didn't equal his belly. He gave his pants another hoist.

'If I have to.'

This time I smiled. 'After you.'

Playing detective was proving easy. I followed behind and watched his cleavage.

CHAPTER SIX

IT WASN'T LIKELY that the dodgy landlord would have the bottle to complain, but I had an oversize guilt complex when I got to work the next day. The fat man's name was Barstow and it would be hard to explain to my boss why I'd wanted to poke my nose into his affairs.

I'd been round the entire house including the room that Thorne had lived in, which was where I'd wanted to be in the first place. As rooms go it wasn't bad, but the brown and purple carpet left a lot to be desired. It had been cleaned out completely, not a hair was left of its last occupant.

When I peered out of the window, three bedrooms opposite displayed themselves brazenly. Two hadn't mattered, but there were things going on in the third that I watched with interest until heavy breathing reminded me I wasn't alone. I beat a retreat, guessing he would be back for the grand finale as soon as I was gone.

Now it was another day, and I had an urgent need to see what Barstow's tax file was like. The feeling I had was familiar; not a regret for having done something, but a fear of getting caught. I'd had it a lot when I was small, it came from spending too much time doing forbidden things.

I was lucky again. Barstow hadn't declared any income from his room-letting, he paid tax on the hundred and fifty a week he earned as a bouncer and that was all. I kindly sent him another form to fill in. He'd like that.

It always happens, every time I'm feeling good and virtuous someone comes along and pricks my bubble. This time it was Nicholls. He wasn't looking at all friendly and he'd brought Detective Constable Clifford with him for protection. Nicholls looked the younger by about five years, and I wondered how he had got ahead in

30

the promotions race. I took them into the interview room and closed the door.

Nicholls started off with stiff formality. 'At four-thirty yesterday you visited a house at 23, Marsden Street. I require to know the purpose of that visit.'

This was interesting; which was being watched – the house or me? I said, 'Why?'

'I have reason to believe that you are withholding information concerning the death of . . .'

'I know, I know,' I said. 'For Pete's sake don't start that again. There's nothing about Thorne that I haven't already told you. How come you don't believe me?'

Stuffily, he snapped, 'In that case you won't mind disclosing why you visited his room yesterday, and please don't deny it, you were observed to be there.'

I wondered where his spy had been and played back the street scene in my mind. I discounted the busy couple across the road, they wouldn't have noticed if I'd had two heads.

I shrugged. 'The world is full of coincidences, isn't it? I had business with Mr Barstow – *tax* business.'

'On a Sunday afternoon? Hardly office hours.'

'That's just about word for word what he said. Another coincidence. Did you follow me to Scorsby Bridge? I had business there too.'

'Can it be confirmed why you were at Marsden Street?'

'By Barstow.'

They exchanged looks that said they wouldn't be asking him. I added sweetly, 'You could always ask my boss to dig into the file. Of course, you'd need to have a convincing reason.'

Nicholls sighed and gave Clifford a nod.

'If you want to wait in the car, I'll be down in a minute.'

Clifford didn't look happy but he went. I waited, hands folded in my lap like patient Griselda. 'You're getting to be a nuisance,' Nicholls said. It was a complaint.

I gave him the lost puppy look. 'And I thought we were establishing such a good relationship.'

31

'If this wasn't a murder investigation and you weren't a suspect,' he admitted, 'I might offer to do better than the police canteen. But since we are where we are, can you keep your nose out of police business?'

'Yes, of course I can,' I said.

It's always best to be truthful. If he'd asked me would I, it might have made things more difficult. I was just beginning to get the hang of playing detective and I didn't intend giving it up without good reason.

'Do you have to see Barstow again?'

'If he forgets to send in his return.'

'Let's hope he doesn't,' Nicholls said. 'No doubt I'll need to see you again soon.'

'You can bank on it,' I agreed, and opened the door for him. When he'd gone I took out the Thorne file and made myself another list. Dates, names, places, just like I'd given to Nicholls.

What I was going to do with them I didn't know, but it seemed as good a place as any to start.

My favourite market trader came in just before eleven; he always keeps his word.

'You embarrassed me, Ron,' I told him. 'In front of all those people, you embarrassed me. Aren't you ashamed?'

'Course I am, love. Don't know why I did it to a sensitive flower like you. Must have been shock. What were you doing there anyway? Should have been tucked up with your boyfriend Sunday afternoon.'

'Your accounts don't disclose a market for Scorsby Bridge,' I said severely. 'Tax evasion, Ron, I thought we'd sorted all that out last week.'

'Yes, well, that's what I come to talk about, isn't it? Just a spur of the moment job that market was, not regular. Woke up, nice day, didn't fancy the missus, thought right, Ron, load up for a bit of grafting, you know how it is.'

He was hopeful and I hated to kick the chair away from under his feet, but since he was providing the rope . . .

'And the week before?' I said gently.

'Now what makes you think . . .?' I shook my head and he stopped and thought about things. 'Jealousy, that's what

32

it is,' he said after a bit. 'Can't sell water to a dehydrated camel half of 'em, should stay home and play with their bleedin' toys.'

'I haven't initialled your accounts yet, Ron; anything you want me to add, any undeclared income?'

'Never goin' to be rich, am I?' he complained. 'Not with snoopy bits like you around. I been doin' it eight weeks, straight up, you can check if you want.'

'I already did,' I said. 'You'll have brought a note of takings.'

He passed me a brown envelope. 'Not a good market,' he said. 'Just a little spurt of trade, that was, when you come.'

I put the envelope in his file unopened.

'Aren't you goin' to look at it?' he said. 'Took half the night that did, wouldn't have done it for anyone but you.'

'Try writing fact instead of fiction,' I suggested. 'I'm told it's easier.' But I smiled to let him know I wasn't that mad. There being only seven days in a week, and having caught him on the seventh, I didn't believe there were many opportunities left to run a fiddle. 'I'll be in touch,' I said, 'one way or the other.'

It irritates me how I'm forever underestimating him.

We stood up and shook hands amicably again. He said, 'Anything I can help with. Grass on a mate maybe and do unto others what he done to me, just let me know.'

'All part of the ball game,' I said unthinkingly.

'Too true,' he said, 'too true, we've got a lot in common, you and me. Keep to the bleedin' rules and kick the right balls, just what I had in mind.'

Why did I have a feeling he wasn't being figurative?

CHAPTER SEVEN

HAVING GOT AWAY with it once it was tempting to try the same thing again. This was probably how crime spread; you didn't get caught on the first job so you did another. Society should be glad I was on the side of the angels.

The security firm Thorne had worked for had its base in a disused chapel to the north of town. Bramfield had a lot of disused chapels, which I supposed was a sign of the times. The old, solid oak door was still in place and I could see the point of keeping it, it would take a lot more effort to get through that than modern chipboard. It stood invitingly open. To the left of the chapel, in what had once been an infants' school, security vans were neatly parked. I went in through the open door and found myself in a reception area that had missed the designer decade. Perhaps the plain shabby look was meant to give clients confidence, if so they should have hired a different girl.

This one looked at me as though I'd interrupted some profound and soul-shattering moment. She took the personal stereo earphones from her multi-pierced ears resentfully. The spiky hair was at least two years out of date, and its bright purple clashed with the magenta walls.

I gave her an official card with my name on it and asked to see the manager. If he did the hiring and firing I was interested to learn what he looked like. She pushed a couple of buttons on the switchboard and talked to someone called Harry. Then she handed back the card and pointed.

'Through that door, up the stairs, third on the right.'

Having done all she intended to do, the earphones went back on. Tinny overflow spilled out, its tsk tsk following me.

On the next floor, behind the third door on the right, I

found a security guard in a nice blue uniform. Someone had given him a holster that almost looked as if it might hold a gun. I handed out the card again. He didn't bother looking at it, just nodded.

'Yeah, yeah, I know; through there.'

Through there was another door and behind it I found Harry. Until then I'd never been sure about this first-name thing; I mean, it's all right to a certain point; egalitarianism and all that, but if everyone down to the office girl is on first-name terms it must make it hard to 'kick butt' as the Americans say. Or so I thought until I met Harry, and after that I knew he could take care of himself.

He was in his mid-fifties and six feet tall with beefy shoulders. When he stood up he was so straight I knew he had to be ex-army or ex-police. He shook hands and his eyes weighed me up and decided I didn't pose that much of a threat. The colour of his hair had changed from dark brown to salt and pepper, and he wore it short. Sometime in his life he'd had a broken nose and it had healed slightly askew; apart from that, in the grey pin-stripe he could have been a banker.

I sat where he told me while he studied the card, and felt like a sixth-former in the Head's study. He said, 'I didn't know we had any problems with taxes,' and set the card down neatly.

'You haven't,' I said. 'I want to talk about an ex-employee of yours we have incomplete records for.'

'Why not ask him?' Harry said. 'Seems easier.'

'Circumstances have made that difficult, he's dead.'

His eyebrows twitched slightly but apart from that he gave no reaction at all. 'He'd been with you six weeks,' I added.

'John Thorne,' Harry said. 'Interesting man. Suddenly everybody wants to know about him.' He waved a hand. 'If you want his work record the police got here first.'

'You might remember most of what I need, I bet you vet the people who work here very closely. Maybe you remember what his last job was, for example.'

'A bouncer, some place in Manchester.'

'That's what we have too.' I tried for a harassed look. 'It's the gap between then and now we have a problem with, nearly six months between giving that up and starting here. I hoped you'd have something on file.'

'Unemployed,' Harry suggested. 'Plenty are.'

Trying for sympathy, I said, 'I will be too if I don't sort this out. Anything you can tell me will be a help, he must have talked to somebody.'

'If he'd needed a shoulder to sob on he wouldn't be working for us. I'll ask around and if I come up with anything I'll ring you.' He flicked the small card with a straight cut fingernail. 'I've got your extension.'

Having failed on sympathy I tried logic. 'You could let me have another print-out, a copy. It'd be a real help.'

'Can't see how, you just said yourself you have the same information.'

'But not his last address,' I said quickly. 'If I had that I could track down social security payments.'

'Why the hell does it matter,' Harry asked logically, 'when he's dead?'

That's the kind of question it's easy to get caught out with. Luckily I had the answer pat and got it out without batting an eyelid. 'It's a simple question of tax liability for his estate. You know how these things are. Mostly red tape.'

He didn't seem impressed. 'Get entangled in red tape,' he said, 'and *wham* you're face down in something nasty.' When he said *wham* his hand slapped down hard on the desk, like he was squashing a fly. I had a feeling it was meant to tell me something, like how low I was to be collecting taxes from a dead man. He stood up again with sour eyes that wanted me thrown out. I moved to the door with him, and tried one last question.

'Just as a matter of interest, what aspect of security work was Thorne busy with when he died? Run of the mill stuff or something special?'

That stopped him, his manner hardened up as he assessed me, his hand on the door keeping it shut.

'What the hell has that got to do with HM Taxes?'

36

'Not a lot,' I admitted. 'Just professional curiosity.'

He said, 'For a tax officer you ask funny questions.'

He walked me downstairs and watched me out of the front door, and I knew it wasn't from politeness. As a detective I'd just drawn a double blank.

Three men came out of the old infants' school and walked up the road ahead of me. Like Harry they were bulky shouldered but they didn't have his height. I followed them, trying not to let myself think that I had nowhere else to go, short of taking a holiday and rushing round the country to all the places Thorne had worked. I didn't want to do that; to begin with I like to spend holiday time face up on a beach.

I turned the corner into Rawcliffe Street and saw the men go into the Three Tuns. A heavy cooking smell drifted out as I drew level, reminding me that sensible people spent their mid-day break eating.

There weren't any empty tables, but the Titus Security men were sat in a window corner where there were two empty seats. I carried over a half lager and a plate of pie and peas and parked my bum on an empty chair.

For an uneasy minute they stopped talking, but when they saw I was concentrating on the food and not trying to chat them up, they decided I was just there to eat and went back to slagging the Bramfield fly-half. When they got tired of that they drifted on to overtime and what a tight-arse Harry was when it came to pay.

I sneaked a better look at them. Two were in their late twenties and I wouldn't have fancied a night out with either, the third was around forty and wore a gold band on his left hand. He it was who said with sour knowledge, 'You can bet he'll forget there's bloody overtime due to Thorne, young Ken here might get paid but he'll not shove money in a dead man's pay packet.'

'So who's to make a fuss?'

'Not the point Jimbo, is it? Could have been you what died, could have been Ken, then what?'

Jimbo thought about it and the tattooed Union Jack on his right forearm twitched, but it was Ken who gave an

37

answer. I couldn't tell if he was into tattoos as well because he wore a long-sleeved shirt, but I did guess at a deep and simple faith in an afterlife from what he said.

'Yeah, well,' he intoned, 'if it had been me an' not poxy Thorne he'd not try it. Knows I'd kick his bloody lights out. Nah. Wouldn't try it.'

There was a minute's silence as the other two took the thought on board. Ken went on:

'That job we was on this nerd comes over, how yer doin' Robby? he ses. Then they both goes off an' when he comes back he ses he didn't know him.'

'Who?'

'The nerd!'

'The nerd said?'

'Naw, poxy Thorne.'

'Said he didn't know the nerd?'

'S' what I said, isn' it?'

'Well he wouldn't, would he? Thorne weren't called Robby for a start, he were Johnny,' said Jimbo, 'so it stands to reason. D'ja know who it was then? Other chap what thought he knew him?'

'Bloody Probation git, that's why I kept me head down. Didn't want him letting on, did I?'

'Letting on?'

'About me having form.'

This too was digested in silence.

'Course, he could have dropped you right in it, couldn't he, if he'd known? Thorne, I mean.'

'Yeah, well, did me a favour, didn't he, an' dropped dead.' With that Ken got tired of talking and went to elbow into the bar.

I laid the fork aside, it had nothing left to do and if I didn't go and get another drink I'd no reason to sit eavesdropping. The other two stayed silent. I was staring into the lager glass when Ken came back. His hands were big enough to carry three pints without a tray.

Jimbo's mind was still on the same set of tracks.

'Pointed him out once, didn't you, when we was down Rooney's. That probo – Ferryman, weren't that his name?'

38

Ken guffawed. 'Nah, he were like that poxy ponce drink, he were a Perry-man.' He laughed again and I wondered if all his jokes were that bad.

I grabbed my handbag and left them to it. Fate had been kind, Mike Perryman and I were old acquaintances. Not the asking home kind but the griping across a lunch table when we'd had a bad morning in court.

From time to time odd bits of information passed between us too, and I had high hopes he would share a little more when I got around to seeing him. I wished it could be there and then but HM paid me to collect her taxes, not play detective. It was really a crying shame how work got in the way of other things. Nicholls of course had nothing to do but solve a simple crime. He also got paid for it and I envied him; with all that time on his hands he should have had it wrapped up by now.

He was waiting for me again, in reception, and by the look on his face I knew that right now I wasn't his favourite person. I was becoming resigned to that.

I said, 'Don't tell me, let me guess. Harry had a word in your ear. Why don't you just move in with me, that way you'll save on shoe leather?'

He didn't smile, and I began to wonder what had made me think he was so much better than the odd assortment Em picked out for me.

I said, 'Look, what is it you want me to do, for heaven's sake – stay home and knit?'

The shutters were well and truly down. He said censoriously, 'You disappoint me, I thought you were intelligent. Harry's ex-CID and knows when he's getting an earful of bull.'

His voice was loud enough to bring Pete out of his office into the neutral corridor where we were standing. Pete might be a pain but he's protective. Sometimes it can be an advantage.

He looked at Nicholls and squared his shoulders. I gave him an A plus. He said, 'If you have problems, shouting at one of our inspectors isn't going to help.'

'This isn't a client,' I said, 'this is pure police harassment.'

I waved the red rag. 'It seems they would prefer me not to look into possible tax evasions.'

Pete gave Nicholls one of his rare, nasty looks. 'Maybe you'd do better talking to me, I can find enough rules and regulations to bog you down for months.'

'And I can arrest any suspect who keeps turning up in the wrong places. You could find yourself missing an inspector.' It was a sour answer, and I had a feeling he meant it, but I could be sour too.

'Who's a suspect, damn it?' I complained. 'All I did was give a little help to a dying man, so why is it I end up being robbed, mugged and spied on?'

I had their full attention. As a display of innocent resentment it was superb and I felt proud of myself.

Pete said, 'That makes it definitely my office, it's time I heard just what's been going on.' He gave me a hurt look that asked why hadn't I told him before.

I went to get the files that would prove how conscientious I'd been, and how sorely victimised. It was a beautiful whitewash job and not until Nicholls had left did Pete suggest a week in the sun, at least two hundred miles from Bramfield, might be a good idea.

I turned it down.

I half expected to see Mike Perryman around when I went to court the next day. I hated that part of the job. Fiddling taxes is a grown-up version of scrumping for apples and gets the same kind of sympathy. One quick look round the courtroom shows who Joe Public is rooting for, and it's never me.

When I'd said my piece I trotted down to the Probation office in the basement. Mike wasn't there but Andrew Baker was in sorting through papers. If you want to know a bad-tempered man, get to meet Andy. I asked where Mike was.

'You tell me,' he sniped. 'I have enough work without getting his on top of it.'

'He's off sick?'

'God knows!'

'But . . .'

'Look, Leah, I'm up to my sodding armpits, find him yourself.'

'Thanks a bunch,' I said and slammed the door.

Probation's main office was ten minutes' walk from the courthouse. Mike might not be there but whoever was wouldn't be as unhelpful as Baker had been. It takes a special kind of man to wear a chip on his shoulder that size. I'd popped in and out to see Mike occasionally and Becky, who looked after reception, knew me.

'If you're wanting Mike you're out of luck,' she said. 'No one knows where he is. There's a panic on.'

'I just collected an earache from Andrew Baker about it,' I said. 'What's happening?'

She pulled a face and shrugged.

'If I believed in flying saucers I'd say he'd been beamed up. Will anybody else do? Fraser's in.'

'It's something only Mike would know, like who he said hello to like an old friend last week sometime.' I realised the time was wrong as soon as I said it, Thorne had been dead a week. 'The week before,' I amended. Becky had looked hopeful but the look went.

'When you said *last* week I thought someone had seen him around.'

Her worry was catching. I said, 'Come on, it can't be that bad.'

She leaned forward.

'Remember, this didn't come from me, but the police are interviewing his clients one by one. I mean, you know Mike – he had real trouble on his books.'

We looked at each other and doubled up on the worry.

I took my share back to work with me and watched it grow. I'd been shouting coincidences down Nicholls' ear and expecting him to believe me, now I had some of my own and I was having trouble with them.

Like how Mike seemed to have known Thorne by a different name, and how one was now dead and the other disappeared.

I chewed on a pen until five o'clock, and then it being Tuesday I went to the health club and tried to work

41

off some anxiety. After that, because I suddenly wanted company and not solitude, I ordered a healthy salad in the coffee cum health food bar and took my time over eating it. Then I sat around drinking coffee until nine.

When I left I was almost their last customer.

Away from the town centre the streets were quiet. I felt glad it was summer, a long walk home on a dark winter's night with a mind full of dead and disappearing men wouldn't have been fun.

Come to that, it wasn't that much fun in summer either.

CHAPTER EIGHT

I WENT TO sleep around midnight and woke just after two to sirens, flashing lights, and slamming doors. There was a faint orange flicker across the ceiling.

I hung out of the window and saw fire tenders at the bottom of the street. An ambulance nosed in past the first of them. It was difficult to count houses in the dark against the curve of the road, but I knew it had to be close to Dora. It might even be . . .

I pulled my head back in and put the light on so I could shimmy into a pair of sweat pants, and shove my feet into trainers. I grabbed a hooded sweat top and ran for the stairs, putting it on as I went. It didn't match but who the hell cared?

Wishing has always been a big disappointment to me. It didn't get me a Wells Fargo rifle when I was eight, or stop me growing boobs at twelve, but right then I wished with everything I'd got that it wouldn't be Dora's house that was burning. It was about two hundred yards to the bottom of Palmer's Run, and when I reached halfway I knew that wishing still didn't work.

The ambulance pulled away just before I got there. Little knots of people were standing around in an assortment of nightwear. I tried trotting past.

'Far enough, love.'

Policemen were beginning to be the bane of my life. I dodged sideways. Oh God it was Dora's. A spurt of flame roof high sparked the little wooden porch over her front door, and a jet of water swung round to douse it. All the flames were coming from the garage and I felt as if I was watching an unscheduled cremation. It was my car in there; the Mini had been

43

old and past its prime, but at least I hadn't owed on it.

I said, 'What happened to Dora? I saw the ambulance, is she all right?'

'Shocked and scorched, precaution more than anything. Go on home, love, nothing you can do here tonight.'

He was probably right, and Nicholls would have been surprised to see me do as I was told. The fire was losing its fierceness but I worried that it was my fault, that I should have had the car serviced more often, that it could have been an electrical fault that started the whole thing off. And when I'd finished worrying about that I worried that my insurance might not cover the damage to Dora's property. As it turned out I should have been worrying about something else, but I didn't know about that until someone woke me again by pounding on the door.

I looked at the alarm clock and its button was down. I didn't remember turning it off. It said 8.45 and if I turned into a crow I might just make it to work on time. The banging started again and I yelled, 'All right, I'm coming, give it a rest,' and got up. I caught sight of myself in the mirror, hair on end and eyes like a bloodhound's. Standing in the minuscule hall I shouted, 'Who is it?'

Marcie said, 'It's . . .' I didn't give her a chance to finish.

'All right, I know, I slept in; thanks, Marcie,' I said, 'come in and have some coffee,' and then I opened the door. I was turning around when I realised who was with her. I wished a brick would drop on Nicholls' head and knock the grin off his stupid face.

The night shirt I had on seemed to have lost at least three inches since I went to bed, I yanked its hem viciously and made good time back to the bedroom. When I came out, decently dressed, Nicholls was in the kitchen. I looked round the door suspiciously and found him making coffee; he looked at the long towelling robe and his face twitched.

'Not one word,' I warned snappily, 'not one single word,' and went to the bathroom to wash my face.

44

He was being busy; the smell of toast crept in under the door.

I scrubbed my teeth clean and went back to the kitchen.

The coffee wasn't bad for someone who had probably been spoiled rotten by a doting mother, but the toast was a little on the crisp side, obviously he needed to get some practice in. I was thinking about that when he told me the fire in Dora's garage had been arson.

My mind snapped back from playing houses. 'Arson as in deliberate?'

'As deliberate as a can of petrol can get,' he agreed, 'and considering the small fact that it was your car, do you get the feeling someone might be trying to get a message across along the lines of mind your own business?'

'Such as who?'

'Such as why, and I'd like to know the answer to that.'

The club had a long waiting list with me at the top. I stood up and said, 'I'm going to ring the hospital and find out about Dora.'

'Sit down, you're not getting out of it so easily. I checked on her before I came and she's all right. Her hair got singed, but she isn't burned, it's lucky she's a light sleeper or the house could have gone too.'

I sat down again and wished he hadn't told me that.

The thought crossed my mind that playing detective hadn't been such a good idea, and right then I didn't want to think about Dora losing her home – who was I kidding? – her life, just because someone I didn't know wanted to warn me off from what, for God's sake?

It was like one of those Chinese puzzle boxes, open one up and there's another waiting inside. That reminded me of something.

I said, 'That Chinese businessman I told you about with the umbrella, have you found him yet?'

He rocked his chair back and stretched, giving me a look that said I was brainless. 'You've read too many spy stories,' he said, 'and anyway it's never a Chinaman, rules of the game.'

45

'Tell me about it,' I said. 'Since when has anybody played by rules?' I sounded annoyed, which was good, because I felt it. 'Remember how the Bulgarian journalist was killed? A pellet of ricin injected by an umbrella? If it can happen once it can happen twice.'

'Leah's law?'

We scowled at each other. He said, 'I know what killed Thorne and it wasn't ricin. Neither was it injected by an umbrella.'

I set my elbows on the table and considered this. 'How then?'

He said, 'It's an odd thing, but in general I prefer it if I ask questions and you answer. What did you do yesterday that upset someone enough to torch your car?'

'Nothing, damn it, except . . .' I remembered the case we were prosecuting right then, it involved a lot of money belonging to a property dealer named Denton, a tall, cadaverous-looking man with lank dark hair and deep-set eyes. We'd eyed each other up in court the previous day, and it hadn't been the biggest thrill of my life. He had a finger in a lot of pies besides property, some of them decidedly seedy, and one thing I was sure about – he didn't like me. There were also rumours that nasty things sometimes happened to people he didn't like. Nicholls looked interested when I told him, but not convinced.

'Take it or leave it,' I snapped, 'I can't think of anyone else with a grudge.'

For some reason that seemed to amuse him. I left him to enjoy the fun and went to get dressed; it was already half past nine and I had a meeting at ten. When I came back looking like a tax inspector in a grey business suit he seemed to have got over the joke. I accepted a lift and hoped the neighbours didn't think I was being arrested.

A little of the clay in his feet became human again when I found he could drive; normally I'm a white knuckle passenger but this time I didn't grab the seat edge at all. He dropped me outside the building and then leaned across, looking up at me through the open door.

'We could share some lunch,' he said.

46

I remembered his last invitation.

'Your canteen or mine?'

'There's a chippy van outside the park.'

'Great,' I said. 'I'll bring the vinegar. One o'clock.' He closed the door and drove off with a wave. Could it be we had a date, I asked myself, or was it all in the line of duty?

I trotted up the bank of concrete stairs. The building is one of those gigantic glass and concrete structures that sprouted like rabid mushrooms during the sixties, featureless on the outside and a rabbit warren on the in. HM Taxes occupied a small corner on the second floor, and DSS a slightly bigger space on the first. The rest of it was taken up by Council departments.

Once they'd all fitted neatly into the Town Hall but I supposed it had seemed a shame to waste the space.

I made it to the meeting on time and Pete looked relieved, the thing he hates most is having to explain things he doesn't understand. When it was over I filled him in on the night's events. The veins were back in his eyes again and I could almost feel the hangover. He came up with the solution he'd thought of before.

'Take a holiday, Leah love, until it gets sorted, we can't risk getting a bomb slung at us in here, can we? I mean think about it, it's a paper mountain.' He tried for the leer that always got him nowhere. 'Ask nicely and I'll come with you.'

'No thanks, Pete, you're too good for me,' I said, 'and anyway I'm not going.' He looked disappointed, he really wanted me out of the place for a while, which I suppose was kind of him considering the amount of extra work he'd have to do if I wasn't there.

Nicholls was on time and waiting in his car. It was standing on a double yellow line and there was a traffic warden bearing down; he hadn't seen her yet because she was coming up from behind, and for a couple of seconds I wondered whether to hang back and see what would happen, but then the nice side of my nature won. I slid in beside him. 'I hope you can do a fast start,' I said, 'or you're booked.'

He looked in the rear-view mirror and saw the eager vulture look. By the time I had the seat belt on we were halfway round the roundabout and cutting up two buses to make the right exit. I said, 'Nice one, and how fast can you go if you're really in a hurry?'

He gave me a grin and said, 'Wings come out the side.'

His eyes were Bunsen burner blue again and I didn't care if we were only going to the chippy, momentarily I forgot the clay feet.

We turned left at the next roundabout and cruised sedately. I had lied to myself about the chippy; I did mind. Falsely cheerful I said, 'Where are we going?'

He grinned again. Silly question.

Within a hundred yards of the south park gates there are two schools, a sports factory, and a wire puller's. The white chippy van was there as usual, doing brisk trade. Nicholls pulled round it and went into the car park. He turned off the engine and faced me. I waited to be told it was a joke, but all he said was:

'Cod or haddock?'

CHAPTER NINE

DORA HAD A rangy kind of boniness about her that I'd been stupid enough to take as a sign of aging. I don't know why I did that, there are plenty of younger women with the same build, but I suppose it's easy to be fooled by grey hair. Too easy. I'd expected to find her looking older and curled in on herself, the way my grandmother had after a bad fall; but Gran had been eighty and that made a difference.

I knew I had gone overboard with the flowers but it was still guilty conscience time, and Dora's face made up for the expense. She was back in her scorched and sad looking house, but not alone. I was glad about that even if the look I got from her daughter Linda implied the whole thing was my fault. For all I knew it was.

Dora's face was bright pink and she had a little less hair at the front, but apart from that she looked fine and no less fit than she had the last time I saw her. She scooped a fat tabby off the chair I normally sat in when she invited me in for tea and gossip, saying, 'Leah, girl, what are we going to do about your poor car?'

Linda didn't give me time to answer.

'Not we, Mother, what's Leah going to do about it.'

According to my dead car's insurers, arson was covered, terrorism was not. I wondered where they drew the line.

Dora threw a look that said she wasn't as pleased at having Linda there as I had thought, and off-loaded the flowers onto her. There wasn't much Linda could do except stalk out to the kitchen and hunt for vases.

I said, 'Dora, my own insurance covers fire, there's no need for you to worry about it.' I looked at her bright face. If Dora was inside and the fire was outside, how did it get that way? I had a sudden suspicion that my good friend

49

hadn't been exactly inactive when the blaze began. When I asked, she looked not exactly guilty, but certainly shifty.

She unhooked the tabby's claws from her cardigan and set it down without answering. The cat came to give me a baleful look and gently waved its tail. Dora lifted it again and dropped it on the settee where it pranced around for a while and pummelled the seat before deciding not to argue.

I said, 'The hair, Dora, and your poor sore face. Tell me about it.'

'There's nothing to tell,' she snapped, 'I got too close, that's all.'

'You were trying to get the car out,' I accused.

'I suppose you wouldn't have.'

'Dora, damn it, I'm . . .' I bit my lip and shut up, what I'd been going to say was insulting and I regretted it. It was also too late already, Dora is a very astute lady.

'Young?' She looked disappointed with me and I felt disappointed with myself. I tried to do damage repair.

'Less vulnerable. Suppose the fire-bug had still been around? I've learned self-defence. At least that's something.'

'And I had a poker. Don't think I wouldn't have used it.' I had an explosive mental picture of her thrashing out like an elderly Boudicca.

'I don't suppose they were still around by then.'

'Then you suppose wrong, and I've already had a lecture from the police, thank you, so don't you start.' Her face seemed even pinker and I realised there *was* a difference in Dora, she was good and mad and I hadn't seen her like that before. It was quite impressive.

'What was he like? Young, fat, thin, tall . . .?' I trailed off.

'Straight out of Crimewatch, right down to the stocking on his head.'

'Fishnet, I'll bet. Did he still have a limp?' That puzzled her. I said, 'Just a joke, Dora, forget about it.' Linda came out of the kitchen with the first of the flower arrangements and I got up to go, time enough to talk to Dora about the

50

error of her ways when her already edgy daughter wasn't there to hear. Dora looked disappointed but came with me to the door.

'If it's any consolation,' I told her, 'I think the fire was directed at me and not you. I hope that helps you to sleep a little easier.'

She said, 'Thank you, Leah, I shall miss you popping round. Where did you say you learned self-defence?'

'The Tai-Chi and Oriental Arts Centre on Pilkington Street, and I'll still be around, you can bank on it.' She looked pleased at that and it gave me a glow. It's always nice to feel wanted.

From inside the house Linda's voice called. 'Mother; you should be sitting down and resting, not standing at the door talking. Let Leah go home now.' She came out into the hall, plumper than her mother, an inch or so shorter, and I guessed nowhere near as nice to know. Dora rolled her eyes.

I said, ''Bye, Dora, take care,' and turned away. I'd underestimated Dora, and I guessed her daughter had done much the same. The difference was, Linda was taking a long time to realise it.

Marcie must have been listening for me because she pulled open her door as I went upstairs and said in a breathless gabble, 'Leah, about this morning, I'm sorry but I had to bring him up he'd been ringing your bell and, well, after what happened . . .'

I said, 'Forget about it, Marcie; it was nice of you to worry, I'd been up half the night because of the fire and I overslept.'

'I slept through it, I suppose because my bedroom is at the back.' She hesitated. 'Wasn't that where you, er . . .?'

'Kept my car,' I finished for her. 'Yes, it was, now all I've got is a claim form.' There was a wail from behind her and she grimaced and went back in. I wondered about being a single parent. Marcie seemed happy enough and I supposed that working from home as she did meant the usual money worries didn't plague her, but I bet there'd

51

been times when she'd wished there was someone else to get up and change nappies.

It was my day for feeling guilty, I'd lived here for a year and not once offered to babysit.

I went on upstairs to my own place and changed into jeans and a washed-out pink sweat shirt, then I boiled some spaghetti and heated up a jar of bolognaise sauce. It wasn't Cordon Bleu but it filled up the gap. The claim form took a lot of thought; the questions weren't really geared to having someone burn down a garage maliciously. When I'd finished I stuck on a stamp and trotted down to the post box.

I'd meant to go only as far as the one on the corner but I found myself walking into town, and posting it at the main box, which I suppose had an unconscious logic to it since that way it would catch the late collection instead of hanging around all night.

My mind had been rambling to itself the way minds do when they're not occupied with anything constructive and, letting my feet go their own way, they took me along Bank Street and past Sam's Plaice where the smell of fish and chips reminded me of Nicholls and his expensive eating habits. I wondered if he'd ask me out again; perhaps next time I'd get to try the hot-dog stand in the market-place.

I came out of Bank Street and took a short cut across the library car park, beyond which a new multi-storeyed horror was going up slowly. Rust coloured steel fingers poked obscenely upwards and Bramfielder's weren't too pleased about it. It wasn't that another car park wouldn't be useful, it was the site the council had decided to build on. There were several fine Georgian buildings close by and a Catholic infants' school that would get a lot of extra lead wafting round its playground.

Then there was the library, built in the nineteenth century but looking as if it had been dreamed up by Heath Robinson with its curlicues, round windows and drunken weather vane. All the extra traffic moving along would be a menace.

The council of course were more concerned with using

what was essentially a cheap building site than worrying their square flat heads about esoteric things.

The builders had been having a lot of problems. Vandals weren't normally cheered and encouraged, but the multi-storey site was made an exception. Any passer-by seeing the odd digger getting itself shoved down a hole whistled cheerily and went his way.

The response had been a high perimeter fence and security guards at night. As I came through the back of the library a batch seemed to have just arrived, spilling out of a dark blue Ford Transit with Watchdog Security written on its side. There were four of them looking like hefty prop halves. One of them was Ken.

I turned right to walk up the hill, and wondered if this was where he'd seen Mike Perryman.

The wooden perimeter fence was about ten feet high and observation holes had been cut out at eye-level so good citizens could watch their money being spent. I stopped and peered through. It was a mess, an oversized adventure playground with plank walks over wet concrete, and grey breeze block mountains. There were still a few workmen about looking macho in hard hats and sweat stains, doing nothing in particular and getting paid for it. When the Watchdog men came in sight they stopped the pretence. I wondered what it was about watching other people work that made it such a draw.

On one square of dried concrete neatly parallel rows of paw prints went from one side to the other, I was glad they hadn't stopped around the middle. One macabre thought led to another, like what a good way it would be to get rid of a body. Drop it down the foundations, pour concrete, and hey presto! – no evidence.

It was a thought I could have done without.

I moved away from the peephole and walked on up the hill. To the right at the top, Goodwin Street cut a sharp tangent back towards the town centre. The Probation office was halfway down.

When Nicholls had wanted to know what I'd been up to the day before the fire I'd told him about the court case, but

53

I hadn't mentioned Mike. Until now my mind hadn't made any connections between his not being around any more and the problems I'd been having. Now my imagination was making links I didn't want to think about.

Over to the west clouds were gathering like pink rinsed woolly sheep. Halfway across the pedestrian bridge I leaned on the metal rail and watched them. Below me four lanes of traffic moved along the by-pass; at this time of night they weren't in too much of a hurry but come morning and they were all Alain Prosts looking for the chequered flag.

A dirty grey cloud skipped in among the clean sheep, leaving little bits of itself behind as it went. I turned and headed home again; I wished I knew what to do. When I got in and looked out of the window the sheep were still there, but there were less of them and the grey cloud was bigger. A wolf had slipped into the fold and the thought worried at me.

CHAPTER TEN

PETE SAID, 'LEAH, love, it was one hell of a night or you're coming down with flu. You look bloody awful, go home.'

For a man with a permanent hangover he had no room to talk and he was wrong on both counts, the dark pouches were pure sleeplessness.

I'd gone to bed tired but when it came to sleep there'd been a difference of opinion between mind and body. Physically I couldn't wait to drop over the cliff edge, but my mind kept dragging me back, it had got itself hooked on a piece of circular knitting, and the fire, Nicholls, the building site and Mike were all part of the pattern.

At two I'd got up and made cocoa and curled up with it in front of the TV. There had been an old black and white movie that normally would have had me asleep after ten minutes, but when it finished at three-thirty I was still with it. I switched off the set and went to crawl back under the covers. Playing detective wasn't as easy as I'd believed. At some point between Thorne's death and Dora's fire, my poking around had really upset somebody. Wow! Keep on like this and I'd outdo Einstein.

Someone, in the little rush of people in the art gallery, had seen Thorne loan me his catalogue, and that someone had tried to get it back. Why? Because Thorne had picked out two paintings?

And where did Harry and Mike come in? They'd both known Thorne but that wasn't any secret. Nicholls knew . . . I stopped on that. Nicholls didn't know about Mike. I rolled over and juggled the pieces around. The mugging and the break-in could be explained by the catalogue, but not the fire – that didn't fit – that had to be Denton's way of saying he didn't like me.

At four the curtains took on that faint grey glow that said the birds would be waking before I had any sleep; I turned my back. A thrush started up; he must have hit on a popular song because after a couple of bars he had a full backing group.

Somewhere around five I stopped listening and five minutes later the eight o'clock alarm went off. The brief sleep hadn't helped any so far as theories went – I still couldn't fit all the pieces into the same picture.

I felt really virtuous dragging myself to work, but when Pete hovered like a paterfamilias I wished I'd stayed home. Damn it, hadn't he any work to do?

Capping the pen I'd been using I set it down neatly and leaned back. This new, caring Pete was unfamiliar and I had a feeling he'd been got at; that being so it didn't take much brain power to work out what would come next.

I was right.

'You need a holiday, take one.'

Smart arse! I tidied up the papers I'd been working on and shoved a little weariness into my voice – it wasn't hard.

'OK, Pete, you win. How long – two weeks, a month, longer? Never look a sick-leave horse in the mouth.' I had him worried, anything over a week always sent him into a panic.

He sat one buttock on the desk and tried a winning smile. The skin under his eyes looked dark and water-logged and said he knew all about heavy nights.

'A week. Go and visit somewhere, put your feet up, stop worrying.'

I said, 'The rest of today will do fine, I don't need a week. I'll be back tomorrow when I've caught up on my sleep. Thanks, Pete, you're a love.'

I patted his hand and left him with an empty desk; if I'd believed it was just Pete worrying about me I might have taken him up on the offer, but I had a feeling greater wheels had been grinding at him, and I thought I knew which.

56

When I'd decided around five that morning that I would have to tell Nicholls about Mike, I'd known Thorne's death might be connected with his disappearance by more than coincidence. I hadn't enjoyed the thought, I'd been trying to stamp on it for two days. My sweet detective sergeant wasn't going to be too pleased when I told him I'd been playing detective in the Three Tuns.

Crossing Market Street I remembered the doggie footprints. I didn't really want to tell Nicholls what a good idea I'd had about instant body disposal, did I?

I trotted up the six steps into the police building and stated my business, then I cooled my heels in the waiting area for half an hour and wondered if he was busy or playing hard to get.

He'd been busy, I knew that just by looking at him. His tie was hanging loose and his hair looked as if he'd been rubbing his hands through it non-stop, and if that wasn't enough his eyes were worse than mine.

I said, 'I'll come back another time,' and got up to go, it didn't seem fair to hang my little worries on him. Head on one side he eyed me critically.

'God, you look awful.'

I wondered how I could stand getting so many compliments in one day. I took a couple of steps to the door. He said, 'There's no need to get huffy, what's the problem?'

'Nothing important, I'll come back when you're not so fragile.' It wasn't intended as an insult but he didn't like it, which meant he must be feeling as bad as he looked. Maybe we both had lousy planetary influences that day.

'You've been up to something,' he said suspiciously.

'Scout's honour, the only thing I've done since I saw you yesterday is spend a sleepless night.' I took another few steps to the door and he set himself between it and me.

'Give me five minutes to finish up and we'll grab some lunch.' I must have looked doubtful because he promised, 'You'll enjoy it.'

When he came back he'd got himself together, his hair looked like it belonged to him and his tie was back in place.

57

We walked round the back of the building, across Paulgate, and turned down Market Street. I thought I knew where we were going, and allowed myself to get resigned to it. When we reached the market Nicholls tagged on to the hot-dog queue.

I insisted we went Dutch, I couldn't stand the thought of all the money he was spending. We sat on a bench across from the gaudy stalls and I hoped nobody I knew would see me there.

The chef de cuisine at the mobile stand had a heavy hand with mustard, but between trying to swallow fast and cooling down with Coke I managed to tell Nicholls about Mike Perryman. Not everything, not right then, just that I was worried he had gone missing. He looked unhappy again.

'A friend,' he said. 'Isn't it amazing that whatever happens we fall over you?' He sounded cynical and cross and I was glad I'd bought my own hot dog. It was no use laying the blame on me if Bramfield's finest weren't up to the job.

'Don't worry,' I said, 'I know you have a lot on your mind. I'll ask around.'

'Around who?'

I gave him a Gallic shrug, then I said, 'I heard CID were going through his Probation files; now you wouldn't be doing that if you thought he was just taking a few days off, would you?'

'And you wouldn't be asking unless you thought you knew something I didn't,' he said with sudden perception.

Across the road from us Ron emerged from the stalls at a gentle canter and joined the queue at the stand. The chef had it down to a fine art; it took less than ten seconds a customer. I tried calculating takings and profit; I can't help doing that, it's just the way my mind works.

Ron got served and looked across the road, he lifted a hand in greeting. I started to raise mine back and saw Nicholls do the same. I let my own drop, it could be politic not to let him know we had even more people in common.

58

Nicholls said, 'Well, what is it then?'

I'd forgotten where we left the conversation, then I remembered: I knew something he didn't know. Well, that was true enough, I did.

I shook the empty Coke tin. 'I think I'd like another,' I said; 'how about you?'

He stood and began fishing in his pocket.

'My shout,' I said, and moved off across the road. I thought he was going to come after me but a couple of carrier laden women were eyeing the bench. He sat down and put his feet up.

When I came back I unburdened my soul, it felt better, a minor absolution. Nicholls choked on his Coke, I patted his back kindly and he flinched as though I'd stabbed him. His look was hostile.

He said, 'You've been withholding evidence.'

'About what? I didn't know Mike had gone missing when I went in the pub. If I had known I would have told you,' I said self-righteously. The lie seemed to appease him, but he did trot out the phrase I was becoming used to.

'You'll have to come back with me and make . . .'

'I know, a statement,' I agreed meekly, 'but in the meantime what do you think's happened to Mike?'

'You tell me,' he said. So I did.

When I got to how the dog's footprints crossed the concrete I think he guessed what was coming, but he heard me out, and when I'd finished we sat quietly on the bench not looking at each other.

Now I'd said it out loud I knew that was the nightmare that had kept me awake last night. As I said before, I liked Mike even though the only time we got together was in court. I didn't want to think there might be no more shared lunches because he was buried under a car park, and I waited for Nicholls to tell me I had imagined it all. But he didn't.

After a while he said quite gently, 'I think we should go now,' and we walked back the way we had come.

CHAPTER ELEVEN

ONE THING ABOUT Nicholls annoyed me intensely, and that was his habit of asking the same old questions. Probably he thought that if he slipped them in often enough he might get different answers. The one he seemed really hung up on was whether Thorne had given me anything other than the catalogue. Picking holes was his job, I knew that, but it wouldn't hurt to be human occasionally and realise I had more on my mind than who gave what to whom.

I said, 'Well, yes, there were a few other things too,' and I ticked them off on my fingers. 'There was a burglary, a mugging, and according to you, my car burnt to a cinder, that's what he gave me, and it would still damn well help to know why.'

'No, it wouldn't,' he said. 'What would help is for you to accept advice and take a holiday; is that so hard?' He was frowning again, someone had stuck a pin in his balloon.

We sat facing each other across a plain wooden table, with a policewoman playing chaperone as though we hadn't shared angst and a bench an hour before.

'Yes, it is hard,' I snapped at him. 'I don't have the kind of job that lets me drop everything and take off.'

He pretended not to hear. 'Keep popping up in the wrong places and people get wrong ideas. A life sentence isn't any longer for two killings than one.' I opened my mouth and he put up his hand. 'I know. I know what you're going to tell me. It's all been a long chain of coincidences. So disappear for a week or two and prove it.'

'Thanks for the lecture, I really appreciate it. Can I go now?'

There was a look on his face I couldn't quite work out:

60

impatience, a touch of anger, and something else hard to pin down. He stacked his papers neatly; he always did that but the folder seemed to have grown since I last saw it.

He said, 'I'll run you home, you should catch up on some sleep.'

'I'm not going home.'

'No?'

'No.'

I could see him itching to ask me why not and I didn't give him any help, it wasn't any of his damn business. Let him worry if he wanted.

He followed me through the door and down the corridor, and watched me go down the outside steps. When I got to the bottom he said, 'I'll see you again, Leah.'

'It's possible,' I agreed, 'one way or the other.'

As it happened I wasn't planning to do anything more exciting than bring Thursday's workout forward a few hours. I knew that once I got home I wouldn't want to make the long hike back into town again.

It was the first weekday afternoon visit I'd made and the health club was almost empty, which suited me fine since it meant I didn't need to make conversation. When I was through, a lot of tiredness had disappeared. I was thinking perhaps things weren't too bad after all, another couple of days and the insurers should be telling me to go and buy a new car – well, a second-hand heap if I was going to be honest, but it would be new to me. And if I stopped being mean I could afford a shiny showroom job; I'd been squirrelling money away for long enough. Taking into account the salary I earned I didn't spend that much.

I came level with the market again. Some stallholders were packing up and going home and it wasn't yet four-thirty. Shoppers were fading away too and the hot-dog stand had its shutter up. Ron had already gone and I wondered if he'd had a good day. I was still thinking about him when I reached Market Street and saw his dark blue van; he slowed down and waved me across, his grin showing there were no hard feelings. Behind him a motor-cyclist was cruising slowly, one foot occasionally

61

touching the ground. There'd been a Kawasaki like that outside the health club when I came out, and I wondered if he was lost.

I waved at Ron and stepped into the road. The Kawasaki's throttle opened up as it came round the van.

I broke into a quick trot, unworried because I knew he had enough room to get round me, but that didn't seem to be his idea. I had almost made it when something painful caught me in the small of the back and the road collided with my head.

According to a lot of things I've read I should have seen stars, or felt myself sinking into black velvet nothingness. Neither of these things happened, or if they did I don't remember them. I do remember opening my eyes to see an ambulanceman bending over me like Prince Charming. His face looked a little fuzzy and I had a splitting headache. He said, 'Don't try moving, just tell me what hurts.'

'My head,' I complained. 'Can you find me two aspirin?'

Then I went to sleep again.

Next time I woke tucked into a hospital bed and my head still hurt. Experimentally I moved other bits of me and found they still worked. Trying to sit up produced a yelp of pain. My back wasn't happy, and the noise brought a staff-nurse crisply starched in blue and white check. She had a look of Em about her, efficient and disapproving.

I let her stick a cold thermometer under my armpit and count pulse beats, and got a good-girl smile. 'You've been lucky,' she said cheerfully, unhooking a chart from the bottom of the bed and recording that I was still alive.

I didn't see why I should agree with her, lucky would mean being at home with my feet up. My knees were hurting in a way I remembered from being small, hot and sore and stiff. I wondered if someone had done the antiseptic bit already; I hoped so or I might just let the side down and cry.

I said, 'What time is it?'

'Ten-thirty.'

Sun was streaming in through the window; something

wasn't right, at ten-thirty it should be setting. She saw the doubt. 'It's Friday morning. You've caught up on lost sleep.'

That's what Pete had sent me home to do; he'd have a field day, so would Nicholls. Fat chance I had of getting out of sick leave now. I asked for a telephone. She said certainly not, first the doctor had to see me, then I would have to talk to the police.

'Why would I do that?' I asked suspiciously.

She was very good at avoiding direct answers.

'Doctor first,' she repeated briskly.

'Thanks,' I said, 'the sooner the better, then I can go home.'

I didn't like the way she laughed.

Lying quietly and trying not to move anything took a lot of concentration, and I knew I wouldn't be able to keep it up for long. It wasn't a doctor I needed, it was aspirin, and then maybe the man working away with a lump hammer would go away.

The staff-nurse came back with an elegant looking man, tall, thin and fortyish, with wire-framed spectacles. She swished the curtains closed around my bed and called him Mr Fraser in the same way she might have called him God. He was used to her and ignored it, why bother with acolytes when there was a prospective convert around.

He said, 'Right, young lady, let's have a look at you,' and gave me one of those medical smiles. I'd decided long ago that the prerequisite for being a doctor was long bony fingers. This one was born to the job. Eventually he gave me the good news that I'd live.

'You've been lucky,' he said, like an echo. 'Nasty bruising and a few bumps. Nothing that won't heal. How's the head?'

'The head is aching.'

He gave me a funny look as if I'd been singing the wrong hymn, then he pulled the bedclothes back up and I felt less at a disadvantage.

'Feel up to talking to the boys in blue?'

'No.'

He didn't seem to understand the word, used as he was to omnipotence. 'I'll send them in,' he said, and left me on my curtained island. I wondered why he'd bothered to ask. He was wrong anyway, it was a girl in blue.

She sat down and fished out a notebook, and asked if I remembered the accident. I said it was unforgettably graven on various bits of me but don't ask about the Kawasaki rider, all I saw was a black helmet. She said witnesses had said it looked deliberate, was I having boyfriend trouble? I told her the only time I had boyfriend trouble was when I found Y-fronts edging into my wash-basket; that had always had a decidedly cooling-off effect on relationships so far.

From the look in her eyes I thought she knew what I meant.

By evening my head felt better and I could sit up and take notice. I was surprised to get a visitor, and not really dressed for it. Someone should get down to designing a new hospital gown. The paperboy had been round selling evening papers and I was looking at a copy half-heartedly. The side-ward I was in held four beds, but it must have been a quiet spell because I was the only customer. Perhaps the aspirin shortage was keeping them away.

Ron had a bunch of flowers and a box of chocolates. 'Well then,' he said, 'that's what you get for giving me heart failure.'

I sniffed at the pink and yellow roses. 'Thanks, Ron, but you shouldn't have.'

He grinned. 'Go down as a business expense, won't they? Anyway, my fault you're here, isn't it? Shouldn't have waved you across. Right bloody villain that Kawasaki nut. Had it in for you, did he?'

'I don't know who he was.'

'Dissatisfied customer.'

'The fourth in ten days.' It came out without thinking.

He scraped a chair across the floor and sat down. 'You in trouble? I know a lot of people'd put that right.'

'Like who?'

He tapped the side of his nose. 'I've got friends in high places, you'd be surprised.'

'Like Detective Sergeant Nicholls of Bramfield's finest.'

'He's Regional not local,' Ron said. 'Thought you'd have known that, being so pally.'

'We're not pally, it's business.'

'Didn't look it from where I was, snuggled up like a right pair of bunnies.'

Bunnies! 'I was not . . .' I caught his eye, he'd been sending me up and I'd bought it. 'Look, in my weakened state less of the leg-pull, it could be fatal. How come you know him?'

'Worked round here before he went up-market.'

'Felt your collar?'

'Take a better man than him. Let's hear your problems then, I've got all night.'

If I hadn't been ninety per cent below par I wouldn't have told him, but right then his was the best shoulder I'd seen. He'd been around and knew a lot of people, some of them, I was sure, on the wrong side of the fence. I didn't care, I dumped the whole lot in front of him, starting with Thorne and ending with the Kawasaki.

'Looks like your boss is right,' he said when I ran down. 'You should take a holiday.'

'Forget it,' I said, 'I'm not the meek kind, and any minute now Nicholls is going to walk through that door and tell me it's all my fault. Do you know how annoying that is?'

'Wife does it all the time. You want to get together with my brother, love, that's your best bet. I'll put in a word, shall I?'

'Who's your brother?' I asked suspiciously.

'Not a villain. Was a DI till he set up on his own; that's surprised you, hasn't it? Thought he'd probably just got out from doing bird, didn't you?'

The thought had hovered in my mind but I was too ashamed to admit it. 'What's he do now?' I said, and had a sudden thought. 'His name wouldn't be Harry, would it? Titus Security Harry?' I thought of all the things I'd just told Ron.

'They're not even mates,' he said. 'When you getting out of this place?'

'No one wants to tell me.'

'I'll have a word on me way out, and if it's not yet a bit I'll tell Tom to come for a chat tomorrow. Give us your phone number, love, just in case. Save having to look in the phone book.'

I wrote it down and gave it to him and he tucked it away in his pocket and left me to myself. I waited for Nicholls to come and tell me I was an idiot. I should have known better: didn't he always let me down?

Chapter Twelve

Hospitals keep early hours, but a six-thirty roll-call seems unjust when you don't get breakfast until eight. By then I'd been given a designer nightie to replace the cotton gown; a neat little number in pink winceyette with a missing button and a washed-in stain that made me wonder who wore it last. It clashed a little with the orang-utan sized, green, red and yellow striped towelling robe that kept falling open.

I'd been promoted from bed-patient to chair-patient which I supposed was a good sign, but I'd have appreciated it more if the chairs hadn't been designed for geriatrics. Sitting in one for any length of time brought on the symptoms.

At nine o'clock a nursing assistant came by with a telephone trolley, and I rang Pete and told him I was taking a holiday after all. Someone had already beaten me to it and he was in his paterfamilias mood again. When he'd finished telling me how to take care of myself and keep out of trouble I said goodbye nicely and wondered what to do next.

I sat on top of the bed and risked rumpling the counterpane; we weren't supposed to do that but I was tired of sliding off the chair's domed leather seat.

Nicholls put in an appearance at ten-thirty just as coffee came round, his timing impeccable as usual. I said, 'You're too late, the murderer was Professor Plum, in the conservatory, with a piece of rope.'

'Sarcasm is unbecoming,' he said primly. 'The RTA report only landed on my desk this morning.' He leaned over the bed and peered at me. 'If you'd let me run you home this wouldn't have happened.'

'If I lived in Bournemouth it wouldn't have happened,'
I said. 'But thanks for the sympathy.'

'What sympathy? I told you to stop poking around.'

'I wasn't damn well poking around, I just went to the
health club, that's all. Anyway, if you're so smart how
come you haven't arrested anybody yet?'

'We're working on it,' he said huffily.

That was another of his faults, he couldn't take criticism.
He sat in the chair and looked comfortable. I said nastily,
'Someone died in that last week.' He got up and looked
out of the window.

'When do you get out?'

'I don't know, I think they're short of patients.'

'Whenever it is I'll pick you up,' he said, 'that way I'll
know you made it home.'

I felt slightly mollified. We sipped from our respective
coffee mugs and I eyed him while he stared down at
the car park. Today he had on a light grey suit with
a blue shirt that picked up the colour of his eyes, but I
thought he could have done better than the maroon and
blue tie. It was a good suit, I noticed, like the ones my
brother-in-law always wore, with hand-stitched lapels. I
resisted an impulse to feel the cloth, he might mistake the
movement for something else. So might I.

Seeing him looking at the car park reminded me of
something.

'Has Mike turned up?'

'No.'

'Have you er . . .'

Sometimes he could be perceptive, he knew I was
thinking about the multi-storey site.

'It's in hand.'

'In hand?' That wasn't good enough. 'Let's forget Mike
and say it's hypothetical. Whose decision would it be to
tear up concrete?'

'Whoever was in charge of the investigation.'

'You?'

'I thought we were being hypothetical. I'm not on the
Perryman case.'

'But you've told whoever is.' He didn't answer that, just looked at me as though I were being unhelpful again. I persisted. 'You *have* told them, haven't you?'

He said, 'Why don't you go and visit with your parents and I'll write and tell you about it.'

Then he came and put his mug at the side of mine on the locker; they looked quite good together, two in hospital blue, even the chips were in the same places. He touched the bandage where the pad of cotton wool stuck out over the stitches.

'Does it hurt much?'

'Terribly.'

'Serves you right,' he said unkindly, and walked away. So much for tenderness.

God came again just before twelve, and I smiled in supplication and asked when I could go home. He poked around the back of me where I couldn't see what he was doing and got a few yelps.

'Not yet,' he said with a playful slap on my backside. 'Give it another two days. How're the waterworks?' I hate euphemisms. I wanted to tell him the waterworks had been privatised, but it doesn't do to get on the wrong side of God. I admitted they were working well.

He had yesterday's staff-nurse in tow, and I wondered if they had something interesting going on off the ward. I had him earmarked as the shiny thigh boot and flagellation type.

At one they dished up a chips and liver super-cholesterol lunch, with ice-cream to follow, and I guessed this was one of the hospitals Edwina Curry hadn't visited. While it digested I cat-napped on the bed and wondered if it would be worth making a run for it.

Soon after five Ron came in. He had a no-nonsense kind of man with him that I guessed must be Tom, and a smile as wide as his face. 'Here you are then, princess,' he said. 'Always keep my word. You just tell our kid all about it. How are you feeling?'

'Better, thanks.'

I turned an inquisitive eye on our kid, who looked to

69

be the elder by five or six years. His hair wasn't dark like Ron's, but sandy, and streaked with grey, and he carried a bit of a paunch, nothing much, just enough to say he wasn't that bothered about keeping fit. But when you looked at the eyes both men's were the same, honey coloured and amused, drooping a little at the corners.

I held out a hand. 'I'm Leah Hunter.'

He took it in a good hard grip, with no half-measures about it. I said, 'Ron mentioned you were ex-CID. So what line are you in now?'

The words sounded prim and I felt vaguely embarrassed, not only that but I was annoyed about unburdening myself to Ron the night before. I knew I had problems, but they weren't something an outsider could do anything about. Besides which, although Ron was someone I'd trust my granny with, sometimes it was easy to forget that most of the time we had a poacher versus gamekeeper relationship.

Tom didn't seem to notice I wasn't brimming with enthusiasm. 'Trust Ron not to tell you the nitty-gritty,' he said. 'Nowadays I get paid to look into things CID have given up on, and between times there's lost moggies and divorces.' He reached inside his leather jacket and took out a business card, it read 'T.A. Tinsley, Detective Agency'.

I shook my head, I was in trouble enough already. Besides, he probably charged a minimum of twenty pounds an hour, maybe more.

'I'm sorry,' I said, 'but I'm not in the market for a detective agency.'

'Did I say you were? This is on the house and between you and me. Ron tells me you've been getting squeezed from both ends.'

I hadn't thought of it that way, but now he'd said it I saw he'd hit the nail on the right spot.

'I'll push off then,' said Ron. 'Anything our kid can't do, you know where to find me.' He gave me a bawdy wink and left us to get on with whatever we decided to get on with.

Tom must have been a wow in CID, he'd got the whole

70

story out of me before I'd even made up my mind to tell
him, and of course he thought it was mostly my own fault;
didn't everyone? The rebuke was direct.

'You shouldn't have played detective. I can see the
attraction but it was a bad mistake. If you take my advice
you'll . . .'

'Take a holiday and leave it to the experts.'

He laughed. 'Had that advice before then, have you?'

I stared down at the glaring terry towelling stripes and
foot or so of winceyette showing below, knowing if I hiked
it up I'd see two knees that couldn't peek out of a short skirt
for a long time to come. That was where curiosity had got
me. So what would be so wrong with taking a holiday? It
was a rhetorical question, and the trouble with rhetorical
questions is the answer stares back, eyeball to eyeball. I'd
always hated to quit, that's what was wrong.

Tom said, 'As I see it, the biggest problem comes from
having some villain think you and Thorne were working
together, but they're not a hundred per cent sure yet or
you'd be dead too.'

That was the sort of thing I didn't want to hear.

'If Nicholls hadn't been so cagey,' I said, shifting the
blame, 'I wouldn't have tried to find out for myself. Why
couldn't he just tell me what was happening?'

'Not his job, is it? You going to tell him about your tax
offenders?'

He had a point, a very good point, but a little less
logic would have made me happier. I should have given
up then, before I asked him what he would do in my
place, and if all my valves had been working I would
have.

He laughed again. 'If I wasn't getting paid for it, love,
not a damn thing.'

I said, 'Well, it's nice to have met you, Tom, but I think
we just reached the end of the line.' I felt disappointed; I
don't know what I'd expected from him, but it had been
more than I got.

He said, 'You're not thinking straight, girl, must be that
bang on the head. I didn't say I wouldn't do anything to

help, did I? I just said I wouldn't have got involved in the first place. All right?'

'All right,' I said. 'Where do we start?'

'We? There isn't no *we* about it, I'm a one-man business and I like it that way. You stay here and pretend to be good and I'll see if I can twist a few arms.'

I've always believed there's no sense in arguing a lost cause; I didn't have any choice at the moment about where I stayed. What I'd do when I got out was a different pan of beans.

I said meekly, 'You'll tell me what you find out?'

'You're the client, you get the report.'

We were shaking on it when Nicholls walked in again. Two visits in one day said something, but as usual I didn't know what. He looked at Tom as if he'd seen an alien from a strange planet. I guessed they knew each other. Tom said, 'Well then, Dave, I hear you've got worries, should have stayed in the little pond.'

'Little ponds get crowded.' Nicholls looked at me. 'What's he doing here?'

'It so happens that Tom is a . . .'

'Friend? It's amazing how all the wrong people are friends or clients. Try again.'

Tom said, 'Forgotten everything I taught you then, have you? Like know who your friends are and keep on the right side of them. I'm here on business, Detective Sergeant.'

'My business,' Nicholls said. 'Miss Hunter is a police witness; there isn't anything she needs a private detective agency for, so you'll have to drum up business somewhere else.'

'That's not for you to decide.' They stared at each other like a pair of dogs deciding whether to fight or run. I didn't think either of them would back off if it came down to it.

I said, 'Don't fight over me, I'm in too fragile a condition; humour me instead.' I scowled at Nicholls. 'What did you come back for?'

'To check you were still here. I told you before, you need a minder.'

72

'I've got Tom, so you can sleep easy in your bed. Unless someone bribes a nurse to slip me a potion, I'm safe.'

'Good lass.' Tom vacated the chair and moved over to Nicholls. 'She'd better be safe,' he said. 'I've got a vested interest and we both know what happens to decoy ducks.'

Decoy ducks? My ears pricked.

'We haven't been using her to flush anybody out,' Nicholls snapped. 'It isn't the way we operate.'

'Things changed that much, have they?' Tom said disbelievingly. He turned and gave me a cheery grin. That was something else he shared with Ron, he had a grin that was an instant pick-me-up. 'I'll be in touch; you need anything sooner, you've got my card.'

I said, 'Thanks, Tom, I appreciate it,' and avoided Nicholls' eyes. When there were only the two of us he came over and sat in the chair Tom had just left. He didn't say anything, simply sat there and looked at me as if I'd become some kind of specimen. I didn't like it. I said, 'Well, it's really nice to have such a chatty visitor, but I think I'll go down to the day room and see if there's anything exciting on TV.'

He stood up and came to the side of the bed, he looked half angry and half disappointed. He said, 'I'll say it again; I've got enough to worry about without having a half-lunatic tax inspector add to it. Spend some time giving thought to that while you have the chance.'

Then he walked away, out of the little ward, and through the rubber swing doors beyond. He was right in what he said, the logic of it could be seen a mile away, but like a dog with a smelly bone, no way was I going to give it up.

CHAPTER THIRTEEN

I MET MARCIE on the stairs, she was on her way down, hauling her son and a baby buggy; the two-year-old had a lip on and I guessed they'd had a difference of opinion. She took a look at me and quipped 'What did the other fella look like?'

'Healthy,' I said. 'Not that I saw much of him.' I moved on up, not wanting to be churlish but not wanting to stop and chit-chat either.

'If you need anything, come and knock,' she invited and went on down. I wondered just how annoyed Nicholls would be to find himself stood up. One of my pet hates is to be taken for granted, and it was time he learned.

When the butt-slapping doctor said I could go home, the staff-nurse gave me a knowing little smile and said she would let my young man know, because he wanted to collect me himself.

I told her irritably that I didn't have a young man, but there's none so deaf as those who will not hear.

Left to my own devices I'd hauled my clothes out of the locker and dressed, folding the pink winceyette up neatly so the stain didn't show and hoping nobody would think it was my doing. The reception area was busy when I went through and no one had taken any notice of me. I'd picked up a taxi from the rank out front and felt clever riding home alone. Now I wasn't so sure. Nicholls made good coffee and right then I'd have appreciated putting my feet up while he got to work in the kitchen.

There was a parcel outside my door wrapped up in brown paper and trying to look innocent. It didn't have any postage stamps, just my name and address written in marker pen. Maybe if my knees had been less like elastic,

74

I might have wondered if it were a bomb, but right then I wasn't at my brightest. When I picked it up it felt heavy like a brick, which wasn't surprising because when I opened it up that's what it was. There was a sheet of white paper with it on which someone with a severe lack of artistic talent had drawn a cat. I left the whole lot on the kitchen table while I set up the coffee-maker. While it was brewing I sat down and took another look at pussy.

I had a feeling the cat and I were meant to have a lot in common; it had a brick tied round its neck and lay in the middle of a puddle. There was a message in thick black capital letters. 'See where curiosity gets you.'

Shit.

I wished I had a return address, it seemed ungrateful not to send a thank you note.

It struck me that some people would say I was having an abnormal reaction since the damn brick was supposed to scare the wits out of me. I pondered on that. Maybe it was the inevitable follow-on from being such a contrary child.

I drew a bathful of hot water and slid in, sipping coffee while I soaked; it felt good to sit in more than a regulation six inches. I'd reached the half-dozing stage when ungentle knocking came on the front door. I guessed it was Nicholls and closed my ears, but eventually I had to haul myself out and into a towelling robe to wet-foot it to the door.

I'd been right again.

'Come on in,' I beefed, stepping back, 'don't wait to be invited. There's coffee in the kitchen, just help yourself.'

He stalked past me and headed for the kitchen.

I went the other way and slid the bathroom bolt home noisily, then took my time giving the bath a thorough clean. It's something I do at least once a year.

When I came out dressed for company he was wearing his favourite scowl; I was glad about that, it saved me feeling guilty.

He had thoughtfully tidied up the kitchen table, and the brick, its wrappings, and the cute kitty drawing had somehow got inside a clear plastic bag.

75

I said, 'It's kind of you to clear the rubbish but I meant it for the dustbin.'

'It'll save you trouble then, won't it?' he responded. 'Hand delivery, was it?'

'Either that or it walked, either way I don't remember making a complaint about it.' I tapped the plastic bag. 'Which means there isn't any reason for this.'

'Evidence.'

'Of what?' I eyed the empty coffee-pot. 'That I have acquaintances with a weird sense of humour?' I set up a new filter and tried to work out why I was annoyed again; he was only doing what he got paid for.

'Anything I say is evidence . . . *is* evidence. That's the way it works.' I shrugged ungraciously. He said, 'Why didn't you wait at the hospital?'

'Maybe I resent being told what to do,' I came back. 'I'm not a fluff brain.'

'Really?'

It was amazing how much disbelief he could shove into one word. I said shortly, 'If you've got everything you came for . . .'

'I have.' He got up. 'Try to keep out of mischief, the odds are getting shorter.'

'Thanks, I'll try to remember.'

Just before he slammed the outside door he hesitated and looked back. For a second I thought he might have something personal on his mind, but if he did he kept it to himself.

After two days at home with nothing to do I was bored out of my skull. Maybe if I was more domesticated I might have had fun washing the carpet, but as ideas went, that never got past the embryo stage. Nicholls hadn't been back since he slammed out. Tom had telephoned once to say he had to go out of town, and would I remember to behave until he got back? I swallowed down a biting reply; men just don't seem to notice how many feet they have.

I paid Dora a visit and let her sympathise with the neat row of stitches in much the same way as I'd sympathised with her scorched face. She was looking better and Linda had gone home again. I suspected Dora was pleased about that. She demanded to be told what had happened and then tut-tutted and gave me a look I was beginning to recognise, so many people seemed to be wearing it.

We sat in the garden soaking up some sun and watched the fat tabby chase cabbage whites. Dora squinted sideways.

'Is intimidation working this time?'

'What intimidation?'

'Ah!' She stuck up three fingers and counted them off.

'A break-in, a fire, a cut head. I'm beginning to worry about you, Leah dear, at my age friends get fewer, I was hoping you might manage to stay the distance.'

So was I, but I shied away from talking about it. Instead I asked, 'Who told you about the break-in?'

'On a cosy street like Palmer's Run news flits from fence to fence. I'd be very interested to know whose pet corn you've been dancing on.' Sharp as ever, Dora had her eye on the ball.

'If I knew I'd dance on it some more,' I said grumpily.

'Hmmph. I expected you to say that. A holiday would do you good, you look decidedly peaky.'

It was funny she should say that. I read a theory once about the way thought waves zip around the ether from one person to another, spreading the same idea; they seemed to be doing that a lot in Bramfield. I swung my wrist up.

'Lord, is that the time? Sorry, Dora, have to go.'

She gave me a knowing look.

'Call in again soon,' she said and settled back comfortably, her old straw with its wide brim tipped forward over her eyes. Dora knew a charade when she saw one.

'You bet,' I said feebly and trotted off.

I rang Pete and told him I felt fine and how about my coming back to work next day. He didn't even take time to think. The refusal was so firm I felt maybe I had something catching.

They say a little knowledge is a dangerous thing, but right then I'd have argued it was the other way around. A

77

lack of knowledge seemed a lot more of a hazard. It also seemed a waste to have so much time on my hands and no ideas. I was getting pretty desperate; as a detective I was useless, maybe I should pull my head back in and stick to tax evaders.

Around oneish Nicholls rang, he sounded out of sorts, but then, when did he not? He said, 'We've got the Kawasaki rider, he says it was an accident and he panicked.'

'It was deliberate.'

'Prove it.'

'That's your job, I'm supposed to be minding my own business. What's his name, anyway?'

'Not something you're entitled to know.' He kept silent for a few seconds then asked. 'How's your head?'

'Bored.'

'Read a book,' he came back and hung up.

I was beginning to feel like a yard dog and it wasn't pleasant. I did some gentle exercising and jogged around the block. When I'd finished, the bruising that looked like a green and purple view of Australia let me know it hadn't enjoyed itself.

About three I caught a bus into town and walked down the hill to the library past the multi-storey site. My intentions were innocent; Nicholls had come up with his first good idea. Read a book, he'd said, so I planned to take home an armful and put my feet up. Again. Only, on the way I got waylaid.

It takes Bramfielders a long time to stir themselves out of lethargy and take positive action, but if the burr is big enough they occasionally do something about it. They were doing that today.

There was quite a crowd, mostly women, picketing outside the site entrance and round about, trading verbal insults with workmen. They seemed to have got themselves well organised with fly-posters giving statistics about lead polution and road injuries to children pasted up on the perimeter fence. I really love it when people get their act together; this crowd had coaxed a TV crew and a couple of press photographers to take note of it all. I got a rare burst of civic pride and kinship and tagged on, it seemed a useful and relatively harmless way of passing the time. One that no one, not even Nicholls, could take exception to.

Except that fate, as usual, took a hand.

When a heavily pregnant woman in a pair of yellow overalls shoved a pole at me and muttered. '*God*, I need a pee,' I took it and watched her make fast time into the library. In her absence I kept my end up and waved the pole with enthusiasm. It was a pity I didn't read the message on its placard then and not when I handed it back. It said.

HOW MANY

DEATHS

BEFORE SOMEONE

LISTENS?

I and it showed up really well on the local TV news that night. Sod's law again. I'd only had hold of the damn thing five minutes, but I knew if certain people were watching they'd give it a whole new meaning.

Mind my own business? Chance would be a fine thing.

CHAPTER FOURTEEN

A CHEQUE FROM the insurance company helped the next day to start out a little better. It wasn't over generous at two thousand pounds but it was more than I'd expected without a lot of quibbling. I propped it against the teapot and regarded it fondly while I ate breakfast. The thought crept into my head that right now a car would be very useful for a little out-of-town snooping. I spent a happy hour trawling through car ads in the local paper; from the number of motor dealers offering 0% finance I guessed they must be having quite a slump.

Pulling on a pair of jeans and a Benetton top – I'd hate some smoothie car salesman to think I couldn't afford his motor – I walked into town and detoured past the bank. I always pay cheques in fast before anyone can change their mind, just a little precaution working for HM Taxes has taught me. A narrow street runs down the side of the bank and a flash Merc was parked at the top; something about the driver looked familiar but I couldn't think what. I didn't waste time worrying about it.

The bank had gone in for designer doors in dark smoked glass with brass edges and push-handles shaped like elephant's ears. They were supposed to let you see who was going in and out, but with the sun at a certain angle they turn opaque. I shoved hard and hoped not to hit anybody. It was a near miss. We stared at each other. The last time we met had been in court, another fortnight and we were due to meet there again. Denton stepped back like he'd come face to face with something unpleasant. I didn't worry about it, sometimes not being popular can be a real compliment.

He put out an arm to hold the door open, body angled so

I had to step sideways to get round him, and when our eyes met the temperature dropped a couple of degrees. Now I knew who the Merc belonged to and why the driver looked familiar, he'd been sitting around outside the courtroom waiting for his boss. I wondered what other jobs Denton had him do besides drive.

When I'd finished my business the Merc had gone, but I still double-checked before I crossed the road. Once bitten, twice shy.

I headed for the Probation Office. I'd decided there was a damn sight better chance of picking up on anything new about Mike from friendly faces there, than from hanging around waiting for Nicholls to tell me anything. I crossed the road and took a short cut down the alley between Tesco's and Runner's betting shop. When I went up the steps and pushed in through the door there was a new girl at Probation's reception desk, who looked as if she should still be at school. She didn't wait for me to say who I wanted, I suppose she didn't think it mattered in the circumstances.

'They're all in a meeting,' she said. 'I can take a message or you can come back later.'

I said, 'Is Beverley about?'

She shook her blonde head plait. 'Not right now, she just slipped out for a few minutes. Sorr-ee.'

So was I, but a few minutes isn't the end of the world.

I trotted to the café on the corner known locally as Greasy Joe's, and got coffee and a do-nut from the counter. Most of their trade is lunch-time take-away. I was heading for the grimy side window where I could watch for Beverley coming back when I heard my name.

'Hey, Leah! Over here.' I knew the voice, I just couldn't put a name to it without a face. Pivoting made coffee slurp over the dinky polystyrene cup and onto the do-nut; I wondered what lunatic genius had invented the damn things.

I said, 'Hi, Jack, long time.'

'Too long, monkey, you should feel ashamed.' He patted the table across from him. Meekly I went to sit down. With

81

round eyes and high cheekbones in a squarish face, Jack gives the impression he got whatever features were left over at the Maker's, but at the same time he does have a certain attraction and a lot of Bramfield women could attest to that. Not me though, he's not my type, and student/teacher liaisons complicate things. He'd had me on my back a few times, and I'd returned the compliment, but it had been strictly professional on practice mats at the Martial Arts Centre. Jack was the lucky owner.

His eyebrows went up. 'Looks like you forgot a few things I taught you,' he said; 'time you got some practice in.' I touched my head, a couple of stitches had dropped out already. I'd be glad when the rest followed suit.

'I've been giving it some thought. Any of the old crowd still around?'

'A few, a few. Gumbo's got his own place in Batley, teaching kids, less aggro.'

'I don't seem to remember you getting much.'

'Ah, well, that's different, new faces get tried out, mine's been around a while, picked up a reputation. When you coming back then? Don't leave it till you seize up. Never mind if you've got bruises, you can start gentle.'

My jaw stopped chewing. OK, I had bruises but they weren't visible, *so how the hell did he know*?
I asked.

'Friend of yours told me,' he said. 'Came to sign on for ladies' self-defence; said I'd been highly recommended by Miss Hunter.'

'Like who?' I said suspiciously.

'Nice old turkey by the name of Dora.'

Dora! Respect grew apace, she was no laggard.

'Well, you look after her,' I said. 'She's a particular friend of mine.'

'I gathered.'

I ran a finger round my plate and licked sugar from it, that's another dreadful childhood habit.

'I might drop by next week,' I said. 'Depends how things go. And I haven't forgotten as much as you think, I dropped a mugger a couple of weeks ago.'

'Did you now? Hands or feet?'

'Feet.'

'Not bad,' he said. 'Got some new boys in, come and look 'em over, might be one of them, you never know. Drop in tomorrow night, back door, private viewing.'

'You know something I don't?'

He shook his head. 'Don't pay much attention to rumours. Have to come and find out, won't you? Round about half-seven.'

'I'll think about it,' I said and stood up. 'I have business,' I apologised. 'See you, Jack.'

Maybe I would drop round tomorrow, I couldn't lose anything.

Beverley was back and alone. She said, 'Hi, Leah, no good asking who you want to see, they're all . . .'

'In a meeting,' I finished for her. 'I know, I already got the message. Anyway you're the one with an ear to the ground, it's you I came to see. Anything new about Mike?'

She took a look around and checked that the PA and intercom switches were off. Then she said, 'I've been specifically told not to talk to you about Mike; don't ask me why but it's police instructions, and everybody has got the same message.' She blinked. 'What do you know that I don't?' The last bit had a plaintive note, as if it was me that knew what was going on while she was in the dark.

I said, 'Look, Beverley, I don't know anything for sure, but you remember the man who dropped dead on me at the art gallery? Well, I think Mike's disappearance is connected to it somehow. I don't know the why and the wherefore, but I do know I'm collecting a lot of trouble one way and another. Anything you can tell me about Mike would help me get out from under.' I fingered my head and it got her attention. Her eyes widened.

'*That* kind of trouble? What happened?'

'Someone with a big black Kawasaki tried to disable me permanently.'

'Tony Murray!' she blurted, then looked upset. 'Forget I said that, it probably had nothing to do with him.'

I said, 'Black leathers, helmet with a Madonna sticker, slim, five eightish? Sound familiar?' I could tell from her face it did.

'Look, Leah . . .'

'I know; you're not supposed to tell me anything, but suppose I guess and you tell me if I'm wrong. He's one of Mike's offenders, isn't he?' She didn't say I was wrong so I took it I'd scored a hit. I said casually, 'Who's looking after him now then, with Mike away?'

'No one, his supervision order ran out about three months ago.' She shrugged. 'That's nothing to do with Mike, is it, so I'm not breaking rules? I'm sorry, Leah, I'd like to help you but . . .'

'I know, but we're doing fine so far. You wouldn't have an address or anything, would you?'

'Only in his file.'

'And you can't get at that?'

'No. Don't ask me, Leah, I like working here.'

'I wouldn't do anything to jeopardise that,' I promised. 'My guess is that Mike picked up on something underhand that got him in trouble, the problem is I'm in it too and I need all the help I can get.' I was laying it on a bit thick but Beverley didn't know that. 'If you do come up with anything that might help give me a call.' I reached over and picked up her jotter pad to scribble my home number on. 'I'll owe you a favour,' I said and left her to think about it.

Back on the street I went in the opposite direction, down past the library to the Fiat showroom. I didn't intend buying one of their cars but I meant to take a test drive anyway, it's always useful to know how other cars handle. I noticed Denton's Merc again, parked on another side-street a bit down from the Probation Office, the driver was reading a newspaper. I took that as a good sign, at least he was literate. When I passed the multi-storey site there were no protesters about; I wondered when they'd be back. There were still fly-posters on the perimeter fence but a lot had been defaced or torn. I took another look through one of the peepholes. Work seemed to be progressing apace and cross girders were being bolted on, there were blue flames here and there from acetylene welders, and over on the left a ramp was already starting on its uphill climb. All the ground-level concreting seemed to be finished now, and no one had turned up with a warrant to dig any of it up. If I were Nicholls I'd be down there fast. But then, if I were Nicholls I'd know what it was all about.

I like the smell of car showrooms, sharp and ripe with polish, leather, shellac and metal blended together. As smells go, it's seductive. I stood in the centre of the floor and sniffed appreciatively. There were two salesmen, one young and looking good, the other in his forties with a dapper little moustache. I hoped I'd get lucky, but instead I got the moustache. He didn't let me go for a test drive until he'd spent ten minutes telling me the policy was for him to drive and me to watch. Stubbornness can be a real virtue at times. When we left I had the steering wheel.

The first five minutes went well, the little Panda felt good and stable, easing up to traffic lights and taking off fast. Of course it didn't have all that much power under the bonnet, but then I don't often drive at Le Mans. I noticed the old Ford Capri edging up close but I didn't think anything about it; there's always someone who likes to cut the distance to an inch.

At the third set of lights it came up at the side of me. There were two muscleheads in it, both in their twenties. I don't know what it is about old Fords, but they do seem to attract the wrong kind of person. These two were making improper gestures and I was refusing to take notice; not so Mr Moustache. He worried about getting the car scratched and told me to turn left. If I'd known what was coming I'd have done what he asked, but it's always easy to be wise after the event.

At the roundabout I moved out onto the by-pass intending to pull off halfway along and cut back to the show-room. I checked the mirror and saw the Capri was still there. That annoyed me. I guessed that if I put my foot down they'd take it as a challenge, so I hung on forty and waited for them to pass. Instead they cruised up and sat on my tail. Mr Moustache said, 'It might be as well if you pull up and I drive back, I don't think it's me they're trying to impress.' I squinted at him sideways. Maybe, maybe not, who could tell these days?

'Pull in where?' I snapped. 'It's a clearway, I'm not supposed to stop.' The Capri drew level and the passenger wagged his fingers at me. I took my foot off the accelerator and dropped back. The Capri did the same. Moustache said, 'This is ridiculous.' I agreed. Exhibitions of macho aggression give me a pain. The Ford edged over until there was only a coat of paint between us. I squinted sideways again and noticed my passenger holding his seat with both hands and looking like he wanted to be somewhere else. I squinted the other way and the gap between the cars closed.

It made a horrible sound, metal on metal. The Panda shivered but held the road. The Capri repeated its manoeuvre then dropped back. A tail of traffic took advantage and zipped past, none of them were heroes. With a mile to go before the turn-off I speeded up to fifty. The Capri went just that little bit faster so it could ram the back end.

Shi-i-t. I shot forward, then back again; Moustache did likewise. Just as we hit the turn-off we got shunted again, then the Capri pulled out and roared past us; both front windows open and two arms out, fingers making a V.

I pulled up and let the car salesman drive us back. He walked round and round the car before he got in the driver's side, and I thought he might cry; if he had I would have understood. When we got back to the showroom I thanked him nicely and said I didn't think a Fiat would be right for me after all. It was a real comfort knowing that this time the car firm's insurance company would have to pay out. I patted the Panda gently and felt sad – it had been such a nice little car.

CHAPTER FIFTEEN

I DIDN'T START shaking until I got back into the centre of town, and then without warning my body started sending out jelly signals. I made a quick right into a café that had waitress service; if I'd needed to carry my own tray I'd have been in trouble. I ordered quiche and a salad and asked for a pot of coffee right away; from the expression on the waitress's face I gathered I must look something like I felt. It was a new experience for me, normally I'm not the nervous kind, but I recognised it had more to do with the five days spent in hospital than the antics of two muscleheads. I drank two cups down in quick succession and started to get myself together again.

The last I saw of the car salesman he'd been heading for the office phone, a little put out because I wouldn't hang around until the police came. It was mean of me, and if I hadn't reached the point of shying like a startled horse when the word statement was mentioned I'd have obliged him. No doubt the boys in blue would call on me in their own good time; since he'd had a good look at my driving licence before we set off it was odds on he'd noted down my name and address. Great!

At the time, I'd been too busy trying to get out of trouble to give much thought to why we were in it. I'm sure the car salesman believed I'd been giving out a come-on, but now I had time to think about it either I was getting one hell of a persecution complex or the Capri was the latest attempt to mess up my life. It was time I got down to some serious thinking.

I'd started out treating the whole thing – not as a joke exactly, no one who watched John Thorne die could have thought it a joke – but as a challenge akin to a crossword puzzle. Face it, I'd felt some pretty strong sexual chemistry moving around with Nicholls about, and I'd wanted to keep him handy. But it hadn't turned out to be the cosy puzzle I'd imagined. I'd ended up with a lot of unpleasant people knowing who I was and where I lived, while I didn't know a thing about them. It was time I got my act together.

I sat and poked at the quiche, it was a small piece and it was going to cost me three pounds fifty, it was also bland, soggy, and emblematic of things going wrong.

I stabbed it viciously and started to run through the few facts I had, and fact number one was inescapable: when Thorne died, either someone among the watchers knew me or I'd been followed home from the police station.

I hadn't noticed anyone on my tail, which said maybe Nicholls was right and I should forget about the Chinaman; I'd sure as hell have noticed *him* trotting along behind me.

The second fact involved two missing paintings of a calibre I'd be ashamed to hang in my bathroom, but both had been ringed in Thorne's catalogue, and someone had been very keen to get that catalogue away from me. I was really tired of asking myself why, but another question had begun to bother me – how did this someone, who seemed to know my movements so well, know I hadn't already given it to Nicholls?

Next fact: I'd become a big worry for someone, and the choice of who had a sore head lay between the fat landlord; Harry; or an as yet unknown player who knew I'd eavesdropped on Ken and his cronies. Last fact of all was Ken's linking of Thorne with Mike Perryman, and the name 'Robby'. Now Mike had gone missing, and one of his spiky clients rode a black Kawasaki. Maybe I should try to learn a little more about Tony Murray.

Laying things out logically was a help; if I wanted to keep playing detective I could see where there might be some leads, I could also see doing that might lead to a short but hectic life. Alternatively, if I stayed home and

88

sewed I could stab a finger and die of blood poisoning, life can be a real shit at times.

I felt better after all that, the puzzle wasn't any easier but at least I was beginning to recognise the pieces. I paid the bill and found a phone box. Tom wasn't back yet so I left a message with his secretary for him to call me. He'd been gone three days and I wondered what he was working on. I didn't think it could have anything to do with my little worries, although he'd copied the list of the places Thorne had worked before he came to Bramfield, and Titus Security.

I'd planned to take more than one test drive, but it didn't seem fair to risk another demolition derby, and anyway I knew that ultimately I was going to replace the old Mini with a new one; the problem was I didn't fancy waking up and finding I had nothing parked outside the house but bent metal.

I took a stroll down Market Street and turned right; another right brought me to Charlie's Car Repairs. With Fagan for a surname his repair shop had copped a 'den of thieves' nickname, and like Ron, he's someone I need to keep an eye on, but taxes apart he can make an engine sing. It was comforting to realise I knew all the right people. Charlie is short on height and porky, with a fringe of hair tied in a pony tail to make up for being bald on top. His sideline is picking up elderly cars and recycling them, and he's shown me some weird and wonderful hybrids. I was hoping he might have one around today, an instantly disposable car it wouldn't break my heart to have trashed. I was lucky, he had a black Morris Minor with a BMW engine change waiting for a buyer.

When I walked around it Charlie grinned. 'Changing jobs then, going in for the fast getaway game?'

'Close, but not close enough,' I said. 'Sure it won't drop to bits?'

'Take it for a run, why don't you? Instant love, I promise. Good sound chassis, bit of rebuilding on the bodywork, and its own mother wouldn't know it. Got a sprinter what looks like a plodder there, love. Go on, try it.'

89

I got in. It smelled of old oil and faint, built-in tobacco smoke, the PVC seats looked scuddy but I guessed Charlie hadn't thought it would matter. The fascia was a nice shade of walnut. I rubbed a finger over it.

'Nice touch that, don't you think?' said Charlie. 'Course if it's not feminine enough you can always put in some chintzy curtains. Depends what you want.'

I got the message.

'No tax disc,' I pointed out.

He gave me one from an Escort. 'There you go.'

So much for legality. Maybe I was too law-abiding.

'Don't get nicked,' he said, 'or I'll swear I never saw you before.' I gave him a rude sign as I drove off. Charlie appreciates things like that.

I kept checking the rear-view mirror but no one seemed to be hanging on my tail, and I had a nice, speedy ride along the by-pass and back. The car handled beautifully, a bit throaty perhaps, but it was a comforting kind of noise like having a well-trained tiger. Since Morris Minors were more or less collectors' items I wondered why Charlie wasn't offering it to an enthusiast, then I realised there wasn't really that much left except the shape. With its new engine and close ratio gear-box it was a swan among ducks.

Charlie said he was robbing himself at two thousand, but he seemed happy enough with the eighteen hundred he got. It was a pity I couldn't drive it away then and there, but there were little things like insurance and road fund licence to be taken care of.

I left Charlie to sort out his end of things; I still had one more place to go. I'm well known at the Law Courts, and that gives me something of an in with the office staff, especially in records where files are whisked in and out on request. They didn't mind looking up Tony Murray for me at all, although being busy they left me to sort through the file myself instead of them doling out little bits of information. I tried to look sad about that.

Tony had a string of arrests and his last court appearance had earned him eighteen months for trafficking. That was

90

interesting; chances were if he had the habit he'd be willing to take on all kinds of little jobs to pay for a fix, even running down pedestrians. I wondered what he was on and noted down the place he lived; it wasn't in the best part of town but funnily enough I knew it well. Thorne had rented a room on Montague Street too. I looked at Tony's photograph; nothing special, an ordinary looking youth with pale hair that could have done with a wash from the way it separated into rat's tails; pale eyes, a long nose. I wondered if I could sneak the photo out of the file without anyone noticing.

They say the thought is the father to the deed. I slid a tentative thumbnail under one corner, it wasn't stuck very well, a couple of quick pushes and the small glossy print almost fell in my lap. It worried me how guilty I felt when I handed the file back, but no one seemed to notice.

From the courts it was only a small detour to reach the multi-storey site. I wanted to know if the protest demo had been short lived or still had life in it. Curiosity can be a curse.

It was four o'clock already which meant school was over. Yesterday the demo had been thinned out when a lot of mums rushed their kids home, maybe they didn't want to risk ideas of democracy getting into young heads; most families don't run along those lines. When I walked by this morning no one had been around, but now the little crowd were back. Someone had pasted new fly-posters on the perimeter fencing; a little more aggravation for whoever had the job of taking them down.

Numbers had swelled. A slightly more sedate poster claimed Bramfield Historical Society were against indiscriminate building. A woman I wouldn't have cared to mess with held another more provocative message: PROTEST AGAINST THE DESTRUCTION OF OUR HISTORIC HERITAGE. I was right with them.

Yesterday I'd had a banner thrust in my hands and ended up a TV star, today the pregnant woman was there again, still in yellow overalls and carrying the same pole. I exploited our brief acquaintance; curiosity being what it is I had to know how the Historical Society had got involved. She looked at me blankly, then a memory cell woke up. 'Oh, I know you, you held the pole while I . . .'

'Right,' I said.

'Right. Come to think of it . . . Would you?'

'Sure, why not?' I took the pole again. Both Em's pregnancies had produced the same effect, every time she saw a loo sign she had to go. There were no cameras around but I hid discreetly behind a large size lady to be on the safe side. My new friend came back and I prompted her memory again. She grinned and raised her eyebrows.

'Oh, well. Somehow they got the idea there might be a Viking site under that lot so they're a bit upset. They've got archaeologists coming from Leeds tomorrow.'

'What put that in their heads?'

'Old coin. No name with it, of course.'

'Isn't it always the case?' I pointed to a stone and brick building twenty yards past the end of the site, until last year it had been a Wesleyan chapel, now it was a mosque. I said, 'It will be terribly difficult concentrating on prayers with all the extra traffic noise. Not that anyone would want to suggest racial insensitivity in building here . . .' Her eyebrows went up again.

'Be terrible if they got that idea,' she said.

'Wouldn't it? Awkward for the council.' We grinned at each other. It's a really good feeling sometimes to stir things up.

CHAPTER SIXTEEN

NEXT DAY I got up early and went for a gentle jog. The morning was pale grey, with cloud cover looking like thin, drifting veils set one above the other. At six-thirty I had the streets to myself and my body wasn't complaining any more, but I didn't push it. I had a whole lot of things lined up, starting with picking up the hybrid from Charlie's, and progressing to things Nicholls would be annoyed about. I planned the day out in my mind and felt good about it. I was also a bit puzzled no one had wanted to talk to me about yesterday's high jinks with the Capri. That surprised me; it was fixed in my mind that Moustache had taken down my licence details. I had a new attack of guilt. Maybe he hadn't, and maybe he'd be in big trouble with his company without a witness to back him up.

Despite the feeling that dedicated detectives didn't waste time worrying about other people's jobs, I called in at the showroom on my way to Charlie's. The reception I got was chilled vinegar. I thought about saying I wanted another test drive, but what the hell, he was already wound up without me adding another twist, so I told him politely why I was there. He lightened up a bit, not much, but enough to tell me something surprising. He hadn't made any phone calls because someone came in right after I left and bought the car. Persuasion didn't get me anywhere, he wasn't going to say who; maybe there'd been a bonus added just to ease his nerves.

Being an amateur at anything has its drawbacks, especially when it comes to prising out information someone doesn't want to give.

Charlie had the car waiting complete with brand new tax disc and MOT, it looked clean and shiny as if he'd spent a half hour cleaning and polishing; I felt honoured, Charlie's usual attitude is take it or leave it. I thanked him nicely and asked about spare keys.

'What you want is a universal,' he said. 'Open anything you fancy then.'

'I don't fancy anything but this, Charlie, but thanks anyway. I'll get some cut.'

'Suit yourself. Seeing as it's you, anything goes wrong bring her back and I'll sort it out.'

I can't help myself, when people are being nice I get suspicious. I said, 'Extra favours aren't on the cards, Charlie, you file a dodgy tax return and I still jump on you.'

He looked aggrieved. 'Did I suggest anything else?'

I said, 'About this universal . . .'

He shook his head. 'Shouldn't have mentioned it, not legal, never know when it might get into wrong hands.' He looked at me with an expression of injured innocence about as genuine as mock crocodile.

'In that case you shouldn't have one yourself,' I returned. 'What are they like?' He handed me a thin piece of metal that looked nothing like a key. I turned it over a couple of times and handed it back. Matching innocence with innocence I said, 'You wouldn't know how to get hold of one that works on household locks, would you?'

He thought about that. 'Might,' he said finally. 'Depends who's asking.'

'You wouldn't believe how often I lose my door key.'

'No, I wouldn't, so don't tell me.' He leaned on the car, looking at me across the roof. I could tell he was asking himself why a tax inspector wanted what amounted to a house-breaking kit. Maybe he thought when all else failed I wanted to do some midnight snooping in empty offices. I hoped he wouldn't ask. He didn't. He picked at a scab on his forearm that had got mixed up in thick hairs. 'I suppose you'd like a bit of instruction on breaking and entering too, sort of thrown in on the QT,' he said.

'If you're offering. Things often come in handy.'

'Dicey.' He took his weight off the car. 'Have a nice

94

ride.' I got in and started up the engine. He walked round to my side and I lowered the window. 'Drop back about three,' he suggested, 'when I've had time for a whisper.'

Maybe in some other life I'd been good.

I'd never been to Mike Perryman's place but I knew it was on the north side of town. It struck me I didn't know much about his domestic arrangements either, other than that he wasn't married. Thinking back over our cosy conversations he hadn't given much away about himself; except that he was a good listener with a wry line in humour. About all I knew was that for recreation he played golf – and I only knew that from seeing clubs in the boot of his car. I wondered which club; there are three in Bramfield, two private and one municipal. I crossed the priciest off the list, I didn't think a Probation Officer would fit in at Thornwood with all those BMWs and fat cigars; everything that went in through the gate was expensive, including – so I'd heard – a few male bimbos.

Pubs and terraces gave way to tree-lined roads. It's funny how you can live in one town the whole of your life and still find streets you haven't been on before. Burntwood Drive was one of them. I drove slowly, feeling at a disadvantage, I knew Mike lived somewhere along there but I'd never had reason to ask what number, and it didn't look the kind of place where I could hop out and knock on a few doors. I got the impression everyone probably minded their own business instead of their neighbours'.

The houses were rustic brick with lawned front gardens well fenced off from each other; solid pre-war semi's with bay windows and mature trees. I cruised from one end to the other and back again wondering if I was wrong about the address.

But dammit why shouldn't Mike live along here? Maybe he'd bought in as an investment; maybe it was his parents' house. Maybe I should have checked the address in the telephone book before I set off.

Once upon a time when I was pre-teen, and telephone boxes were pre-vandal, they had directories in them. Now they just smelled of urine and didn't work. A post office van turned onto the Drive and went the opposite way; I did a quick three point and followed. It stopped halfway along and the driver got out with a parcel; when he came back from his delivery I was waiting for him. I put on my best smile and said how silly it was, I'd forgotten my friend's house number. He told me it was something he did all the time, and this wasn't his route so he couldn't help me. He put on what I guessed was his best smile while he said it.

I went back to the hybrid and sat in it feeling frustrated. Why didn't I just knock on a door and ask to look at a telephone directory? Why? Because I was scared of looking like a gerbil, that's why.

I'd just started up the engine, when a woman clip-clopped towards me from the house where the postman had just made his delivery. She looked in her mid-sixties, plump and pleasant with a blue rinse on her hair. I turned off the ignition and got out again.

She stopped two or three feet away. 'Are you having trouble finding an address?'

'Mike Perryman, I forgot his house number.'

She pointed across the road diagonally. 'That's where you want to be, number fifty-four, but I'm afraid it's a waste of time, he isn't home.'

I smiled brightly. 'Oh well, maybe I can wait.'

'I don't think so, dear, no one seems to know when he's coming back.' She looked at me doubtfully. 'There's some sort of police inquiry going on, we're all very puzzled about it, the house has been searched and the neighbours questioned. Very upsetting, really.' She stared at the black front door of Mike's house as if he might suddenly appear and explain everything.

'Unsettling,' I agreed. 'What kind of questions?'

'Comings and goings, visitors to the house – not the kind of thing one really notices very much.'

I swallowed down a smile. I could take her to some streets where noticing was a lifetime's occupation.

I said, 'Yes, well, I can understand that, and I know

96

Mike liked to keep his private life separate from the job. I suppose on a quiet street like this noise would be noticed more than people.'

'Especially at two in the morning,' she said thoughtlessly and coloured when she caught my eye. 'Motor bikes create a dreadful din. I remember one leaving several nights in succession about a month ago.'

'Did you get a sight of it?'

There was a string of white beads at the neck of her blue lawn print dress. Her fingers reached up and played with them while her eyes suddenly avoided mine, I remembered that she'd probably been asked too many questions already, by other people. I shared a confidence.

'I know a client of Mike's owns a black Kawasaki, but I'm not sure if Mike would invite him home, it isn't something he normally did.' Most of that was pure invention. I didn't know if Mike had clients home or not; what I wanted was to move myself from interrogator to confidante and keep her talking. It seemed to work, the fingers stopped playing and her eyes came back to me.

She said, 'I didn't know him well enough to ask his profession, but someone mentioned social work.'

'Probation,' I told her obligingly. 'Difficult work. Did you get a look at the motor bike?'

'I've no idea what colour it was, everything looks the same under orange street lights.' I was disappointed, I didn't want to be told all cats were grey in the dark. Then she said suddenly, 'There is one thing I remember, I saw him put on his helmet under the street light and his hair was pale. Does that sound like Mr Perryman's client?'

'Yes,' I said feeling pleased with myself. 'Yes, it does.' I wasn't sure how the knowledge that Tony Murray had probably visited Mike at home would help, but it was a new fact to add to my little list. I smiled gratefully. 'Thanks,' I said kindly, 'you've been a big help.'

97

As I started to get back in the car she said, 'Who can I say was looking for him if anyone asks?'

'Just a friend on a courtesy call.'

'But . . .'

I gave her a cheery wave and drove back the way I'd come.

CHAPTER SEVENTEEN

I DIDN'T GO home mid-day and maybe that was a mistake, because sometime during my gallivanting an unfriendly person messed with my flat again. This time it was a neat precision job and I'd helped it along by not having the locks changed. I was ignorant of all that when I pulled into a parking spot and trotted into the Three Tuns. Daniel had nothing on me, his lions were a pushover. I ordered pie and peas and looked around for a likely spot to sit.

The first ear-flapping session had been profitable enough to raise hopes for more. The place wasn't as crowded as last time and it was hard to guess which if any eaters worked for Titus Security. I'd been hoping Ken and his cronies might be there. Not knowing how Harry's shift system worked was a definite drawback.

Since there were empty tables around it would be hard to butt in on somebody else's party, and I felt put out about that, as if fate and I should have been on better terms. I settled on a table for two by the window, squashed between two that were both bigger and occupied. Maybe I'd get lucky, if not – well I had to eat somewhere.

It was a good thing I was philosophical, because what I picked up was a lot of gossip about people I'd never heard of, but not a thing that concerned me.

I drank three non-alcoholic lagers and sat there for an hour. By two the place was almost empty and I gave up and went back to the hybrid. Mike Hammer never drew a blank – not on my TV set he didn't.

Charlie had said drop back around three, and with time left to kill I wandered round the market. The cloud veils had burnt back and there was now only a thin layer covering the sun; it felt warm and gentle. Ron's patter was drawing crowds as usual and I elbowed my way to the front to ask about Tom. I got a look of approval.

'That's what I like,' he said. 'Bouncing balls, *nil desperandum* and all that. Tom's back, love, I'll tell him you asked.' Then he gave me his usual wink and went back to selling calories.

Just before three I drove into Charlie's yard. A long time ago the place had been the local ostler's with a row of stables and a bigger ramshackle building you could get a couple of carriages in. The stables had fallen to bits years back but the main building had been patched up by Charlie. He'd laid himself a concrete floor and slung a corrugated roof on to replace the old stone tiles; I could see the sense in that, the old wooden roof frame was rotten enough to let a couple drop on some fool's head.

The inspection pit was open and an old Cortina straddled it, a yellow light showed underneath. I parked and walked over. It goes without saying that Charlie doesn't run to such modern wonders as a hydraulic ramp so I squatted on my haunches and peered down. A stream of dirty oil gushed out; I admired the neat way he shoved a battered can under and didn't miss a drop. I said, 'Any luck?'

'Have a sit in the office,' he said. 'Shan't be two ticks, put the kettle on if you like.' I accepted the honour in silence, I knew Charlie's lean-to office well, chaos would be another name for it and the smell wasn't too good either. Grease, tobacco, sweat and mildew make a lethal cocktail. I put the kettle to boil and went to sit on the step; that way I could breathe in everyday polluted air and kid myself it was healthy.

After a bit Charlie came, wiping his hands on a rag that wasn't doing its job. 'Might have got you fixed up,' he said. 'Want a cup of tea then?'

'Why not?' I said, sitting firm as he stepped past me. It might be a close thing but his tea hadn't killed me yet. I didn't offer to be mother. When he'd brewed up we sat amicably side by side and he told me a few points of law. I suppose it was for the good of my soul but it surprised me; Charlie as crime preventer was like Winnie the Pooh

100

as honey warden. His lecture was brief and all about how the making and selling of picklocks isn't illegal, and neither is owning and carrying, but the roof falls in if you get caught on someone else's property. He sounded like my father warning me about men and life and wickedness. I really appreciated it.

I said, 'OK, Charlie, thanks, but I don't plan to rob any banks. How about letting the customer see what she's buying.'

He blew his nose into the rag he'd wiped his hands on, and his nose took on a dark sheen. That's another thing I like about Charlie, he has such endearing habits. 'Not much use having summat you don't know what to do with, is it?' he asked pragmatically. 'Drop round Sid's after Sunday dinner an' he'll see you right.'

Sid's. Did I know a Sid? I did not. 'Sid who?'

He got up and turned into the office. Surreptitiously I tipped what was left of the tea onto a tuft of grass; a little stream escaped and I scuffed at it guiltily. 'Grundy Street,' Charlie said, dropping down at the side of me again. 'Number five.'

Grundy Street was in a part of Bramfield the city fathers were ashamed of, so much so they'd been busily demolishing everything in sight and levelling it off. I said mildly, 'I thought it had been pulled down.'

'Course it has, s'why I'm sending you there.' He gave me a squinty look. 'Lives down a drain, doesn't he, bloody teenage mutant turtle. Lead balls haven't got round to Grundy Street yet. Want another pot of tea?'

'No, thanks,' I said hastily. 'Appreciated though.' I really was an awful liar.

Driving home I kept a close watch on the rear-view mirror, and when I got to Palmer's Run parked on the opposite side of the street; that way I could keep an eye on my property and still hope no one with a grudge would guess the little black car was mine. All right, I'd bought it to be instantly disposable, but that didn't mean I'd actually enjoy having it trashed.

I let myself into the flat and closed the door behind me.

101

Then I stood still and looked around; something seemed to be different about the feel of the place. Quietly I slipped back the latch and opened the door again, leaving it that way while I took a look around. Nothing was out of place and no one jumped out from the broom cupboard or under the bed. I told myself I was getting too jumpy to live with and went back to close the door. When the telephone rang I shot about a foot in the air.

It was Tom.

He said he had a lot to tell me and how about him coming round next day about three. I told him fine I'd have the kettle on. Clairvoyant I'm not. I messed around for a bit, then I put my feet up and listened to some music and thought about what a great time I was having.

I got to the Martial Arts Centre soon after seven. By a pleasant coincidence it stands next to a pub, which is nice all round; Jack gets to share the car park and the pub gets to slake the thirsts all that aggressive activity creates. I slid in neatly between a fat old Volvo and a big Toyota; sideways on the hybrid was almost invisible. Jack keeps the back door locked; it's a sad fact of life that you can't trust anyone these days, especially around an equipment room. The room itself carried a big enough notice: THIS DOOR MUST BE KEPT LOCKED AT ALL TIMES, but like the man said, between the thought and the deed falls the shadow.

I rang the bell and waited. I hadn't given Jack's half-hinted revelation much thought, but turning my mind to it now I knew that I wouldn't recognise the mugger even if he came up and shook my hand. When I stepped in through the door I felt nostalgic. I'd really enjoyed throwing people around. Jack said, 'Couldn't resist the peep-show then?' and gave me a good look-over. 'Been doing anything to keep in shape?'

'A few health club work-outs.'

'Good, won't hurt as much Monday then, will it? Ladies' night.'

'I didn't say I'd come.'

'Payment for the royal box tonight, monkey.' I followed him into his office and blinked. Last time I'd been there he'd

102

had an observation slot about six by ten inches, now he had a window six feet by four. From his point of view it was a great improvement, he could see what was happening in the practice room without getting out of his chair, but conversely they'd all know he was watching them. Or so I thought before he enlightened me.

'Don't worry,' he said, 'it's all down to the wonder of science. Can't see a thing from out there, other side's a mirror. Should get a good laugh, pose round like bantam cocks, half of 'em. Settle down and watch; want some coffee? Help yourself.'

He left me alone and went to spread the mats. At half past seven the new boys appeared. I can't say they looked self-conscious in their white pyjamas because it was something else entirely, more an awareness that the kit gave them an extra machismo. I watched Jack take them through their paces. Maybe thuggy was among them, if so I didn't recognise him. I recognised someone else though: the last time I'd seen him he had his arm out of a Capri window and two fingers up.

After twenty minutes Jack called a breather and came to see how I was doing. He was interested to hear about the fun I'd had on the test drive.

He said, 'He's a naughty boy that one, very naughty, and he's had his hand slapped; thought he was supposed to have turned over a new leaf.'

That sounded really promising. I said, 'What's his line of work then? Anything interesting?'

'Depends what you call interesting, he does any little job his boss asks him to do. Regular pooper-scooper is our Kevin.'

'Does his boss have a name?'

'A man you should keep away from, love. Bramfield's own public benefactor, James Aloysius Denton. Heard of him, I suppose.'

'Have I not?' I said hollowly. 'HM Taxes just happen to be carrying on a current prosecution.'

And who, I asked myself, was the star witness?

'Well,' he said. 'That explains a lot, doesn't it?'

103

It did and it didn't, either way it gave me a lot to think about.

Coincidences were a pain but they happened; I'd linked most of my troubles to the death of John Thorne, but suppose I was wrong, suppose he and Mike were the coincidences, and the real cause of the fun-time I'd been having was my being a pain in Denton's ass. I thought about the flat grey eyes that had met mine at the bank, the Merc waiting outside.

It had been holed up near Probation too, and no doubt the latest technology in car phones could have kept Denton in touch with what I was up to. Easy now to see how the Capri homed in on me, and who but Denton would have paid for a battered Fiat? And probably given Moustache that little extra for his fright.

It was an unpleasant feeling to know I'd been followed so effectively and without knowing a thing about it.

I drove home and parked across the street again, then I made good time into my flat and dropped the deadlock. I was really getting safety conscious. I heated up a curry from the freezer and ate it in front of the television. My ears were pricked like a cat's, and I got another urge to look under the bed.

I'd really have to do something about the fluff.

CHAPTER EIGHTEEN

IT'S FUNNY THE way things work out. When I got up
from my bed next morning I was about ready to send the
bloodhound home and put the magnifying glass away. In
other words, talking to Jack had given my psyche a cold
shower. Everything, from breaking up my flat to teaching
me about road safety, could be given a logical, Thorne-less
explanation. It was time to stop playing detective. With me
up front as ace trouble-shooter, HM Taxes had Denton
by the short and curlies, in return, true to reputation, he
was giving me aggro. So be it. I'd pass the news on to
Nicholls, but I bet he sure as hell wouldn't be able to prove
a damn thing.

That's the way I planned to do things, but isn't it always
the truth that some people never know when to leave
well alone?

It had got to Saturday again and by rights I should have
been heading for the park, instead, my newly obedient
frame of mind settled for what the doctor ordered and cut
down to an easy two-mile run through the quiet streets.
I gave myself a gold star. It was so good to be virtuous
and do what Nicholls had wanted in the first place – let
him handle things in his own sweet way.

Fat chance!

Back home I took a shower and pulled on jeans and an
Amnesty T-shirt; the T-shirt had a barred window on the
back of it and as things turned out it was a good choice. I
swear that right after breakfast I was going to drive down
to the police station and tell Nicholls all about it, but he
spoiled things as usual. I don't know where he'd picked
up the habit of knocking that hard on the door but it
irritated me. I took my time. The pounding came again.

When it stopped I heard fractious toddler noises from downstairs. Great!

I yelled, 'All right, I'm coming. Who wants me?'

'Detective Sergeant Nicholls. Open the door.'

He sounded officious and overly so. I wondered what I was supposed to have done this time and got a warm feeling when I thought how wrong he had to be. I'd reformed, I was now a good and obedient citizen. Then I pulled open the door and got the first little flutter of alarm. He'd brought the unfriendly looking Detective Constable Clifford with him, and a WPC for back-up.

They pushed past me and Nicholls flapped a folded piece of paper in front of my eyes.

'Read it,' he snapped. 'It's a search warrant.'

'For what, for God's sake? I sold the Crown Jewels last week, you're too late.' He gave me a drop-dead look and I felt hurt. I said, 'Well, feel free,' then I scrumpled up his nice paper and stuffed it in his pocket.

I went back to the kitchen and the WPC came with me. She had a quiet voice, not the kind to quell a riot. She said, 'You shouldn't have done that, he wasn't in a good mood to start with.'

Tough!

I got on with eating. The WPC's nut-coloured hair was nice and shiny and curled up round the sides of her cap. I guessed she was two or three years younger than I was; that made me feel old. I said, 'What's he looking for anyway?'

'He didn't tell me.'

'Wouldn't you know it? I think he has some deep-seated psychological problem the way he likes to keep things close to his chest.'

She didn't answer that. I hate it when people don't want to exchange small talk. I finished up and rinsed the pots. Maybe on their way round someone would make the bed for me; this would teach me not to be messy.

From the noise Nicholls and Clifford made, they were doing a thorough job. I went to watch, you can't be too careful, a person only has to read the tabloids to realise that. Nicholls and his little helper were in the bedroom, and – ho hum – after today's little episode that was as near as the good detective sergeant was ever likely to get.

I said kindly, 'If I knew what you were looking for I could tell you where it is.' Activity ceased and two heads swivelled to look at me. I couldn't decide which held the most suspicion.

Clifford growled, 'We need a step-ladder, where do you keep it?'

It wasn't the question I'd been expecting, especially since he'd been rummaging through my undies drawer right before he asked. He had a pair of black satin briefs in his hand with little red bows down the lace front. They weren't the kind of thing I would normally wear, and they'd come packaged in a ring-pull can. It was Pete's idea of a jokey Christmas present. I looked at them thoughtfully.

'I've heard about knicker fetishism,' I sympathised, 'is it much of a problem?' He went red and his eyes turned piggy. I added a modicum more fuel. 'Keep them if you want, I shan't mind.' I wondered if he had a blood-pressure problem; maybe that was why he'd been passed over for promotion.

Nicholls stepped in between us and cut off my view. He said shortly, 'Step-ladder.'

I trotted back to the kitchen and pulled the three-step from its hiding place. He looked a bit non-plussed. 'That's it?'

'That's it,' I agreed.

Standing on top he was short of reaching the ceiling by an inch; these old houses weren't built for pygmies. He got down. 'So how do you get into the roof space?' he said acerbically.

'What roof space?'

He grabbed me by the elbow and did a quick hustle into the bathroom. Standing on my pretty pink carpet he jabbed a finger upwards 'That roof space.'

We both looked at the trap-door. Of course I'd known it was there but I couldn't think of any eventuality that would make me want to go through it. I'm not exactly arachniphobic but I wouldn't go looking for the little brutes. I told him that, but he didn't seem to believe me. Clifford came in and they had a debate about it.

I said, 'If you really want to have a look up there try a chair on the kitchen table.' I folded my arms and leaned comfortably. This might be good.

The table was old pine with a top two inches thick and the kind of chunky legs Victorians liked to put on everything. I guess when you think about it they needed security symbols. It would take a hernia or two to get it in the bathroom. But Nicholls was no mental slouch, it didn't take him any longer than an earthworm to figure out I couldn't have climbed into the loft that way myself, alone and unaided. Of course I could have pointed that out in the beginning, but why spoil his fun?

Having got hold of the pyramid idea they looked around for something easier, but since the rest of the stuff is mostly fitted or ladder-rack to save on space they didn't have much luck. After a bit Nicholls sent Clifford out to borrow a step-ladder, I didn't think many of the neighbours would be home but the words of wisdom fell on deaf ears. While we hung about waiting I tried coaxing a little information, but Nicholls wasn't talking.

It took a while for Clifford to find an old set of steps I wouldn't have trusted my life to, but Clifford obviously didn't value his own that highly. When he shoved the trap-door back a puff of dust came through. He poked around, head and shoulders through the hole, and the uneasy feeling came back: I remembered how I'd sensed something alien about the place when I got home the day before – as if it had been violated again.

It had.

Nicholls didn't look happy about what they found, I have to grant him that. It was the first time I'd ever had my rights read out and it was an unnerving experience. This time I didn't interrupt, I left him to finish all by himself. There wasn't a lot I could say considering that Clifford had climbed back down from the hole with *Blue Nude with*

108

Carnation, and *Autumn Woods on a Wet Day* clutched in his hot little hand. I knew the big question I was going to be asked was what they were doing in my roof space, and I really wished I knew the answer.

When we filed onto the street I tried to look innocent. I hoped I'd been right about the neighbours not being around, if this kind of thing kept up I'd be classed as an undesirable. I rode to town in the back seat of the Sierra, and Nicholls put on a strong and silent act in the front that rubbed off on the WPC at my side. I wished somebody would talk to me. By the time we got to the police station the chill factor had gone up considerably.

I'd grabbed my shoulder-bag before we left and I didn't enjoy handing it over and having it tipped out, but there was too much muscle around to make it an issue. At least when they'd finished I got a private waiting room, but it was a shame they hadn't done more to make it cosy. It wasn't nice to sit on a hard bench and watch the little window in the door slam shut.

Being banged up in a cell was just one more experience I could do without.

After a bit I started to get good and angry again. If this was Denton's doing he had to be slipping, it tied him in with Thorne's messy exit and I didn't think he was that stupid. But the business with the Capri had been his idea, that I was sure about. And what about Dora's garage? I did a rapid reassessment.

The test drive had been hairy but not that dangerous, not so the Kawasaki stunt, that could – *should?* – have been deadly. Certain implications hung on that, and I gave them some careful thought. Did I still believe Denton was behind everything?

Did I believe the moon was made from green cheese?

It felt really good to be back with not one, but two villains on my back. Last time I'd floated that idea past Nicholls he hadn't been impressed; I wondered if he'd handle it any better this time. I was feeling disappointed in the good detective sergeant, but I guessed that right then he felt the same about me.

I'd no way of knowing how long I'd be left sitting around to contemplate my sins, such as they were. Way back when, my Gran used to say I had meddling fingers and a pokey nose, and in my formative years the fingers came in for quite a few slaps. I never had seen it that way myself, being born with an insatiable curiosity wasn't exactly my fault.

I watched two flies copulate on the ceiling, they took a long time about it.

At twelve-thirty I got corned beef and chips on a paper plate. It was a wordless delivery and the fork was plastic. I wondered if they had me marked down as dangerous; it was a worry that didn't stop me cleaning the plate like a good little convict who didn't know when her next meal might come by.

Having so much time to think had brought one thing into sharp focus. Someone had done a neat sewing job and if I couldn't unpick the stitches I was in real trouble.

CHAPTER NINETEEN

THERE'S SOMETHING VERY deflating about being escorted to the lavatory, it took me right back to kindergarten and that quaint musty smell of wet pants and hot radiators. I'd made the trip twice before Nicholls got around to talking to me and I'll tell you right now, having nothing to do but stare at a wall isn't exactly stimulating.

I guessed the long wait was supposed to be a softening-up process. I was grateful to the flies – in every great plan there's a flaw.

From the way he kept repeating questions Nicholls seemed to have a big problem with his short-term memory. It irked me, and with a boredom threshold already on overload it was tempting to vary the answers a bit, but then again I didn't want to stay around talking any longer than I could help. After half an hour he seemed to accept that if I wasn't telling the truth about not knowing how the paintings got in my loft, I was too good a liar for him to beat. One thing I knew, the minute I was out of there I was heading for a locksmith.

He turned off the tape-recorder and got a dirty look from Clifford. Maybe that was why he sounded so peevish.

'I'd like to slam you in a cell and forget where I put the key, so get out of here, Leah, before I do it. Just one thing. If you're away from home more than twenty-four hours I want to know about it beforehand. Is that understood?'

'Perfectly.'

Nicholls' problem was not knowing how to handle people. I could have told him a lot of interesting things if he hadn't gone out of his way to make me mad. It's amazing how fast good intentions can go down the tubes; only this morning I'd woken up wanting nothing more

111

than to be a good little citizen and here I was again hackles up and ready to bite.

He said, 'About this intruder business, I thought you'd agreed to keep the street door locked.'

'A chain is only as good as its weakest link,' I reminded him self-righteously, 'and I'm not the only one who lives there. Talking of which I'm getting the locks changed, so any old keys you have lying around don't expect them to fit.'

Clifford gave him squinty appraisal at that, but what did I care if he needed to clean his mind out? Or maybe he knew more about Nicholls' habits than I did. Maybe there was a whole bunch of keys lying around.

Nicholls said, 'If I fall over you again I'll arrest you for your own good.'

I smiled sweetly. 'You can't.'

'Try me.'

'What grounds?'

'Obstruction of police inquiries.'

Like a pair of circling dogs we eyed each other and I wondered who would get the last bite. He probably meant what he said. Well, sod him. Why should I roll over just to make his life easier? I folded my arms and sat comfortable. 'I'll let my solicitor know, that way he'll be expecting a call.'

Nicholls broke a habit: this time when he stood up he didn't bother straightening his papers, he just slammed the file closed and strode out of the room.

Tough!

I turned my attention to Clifford. 'Well, I hate to be the one to break up the party,' I said, 'but there are a few little things I'd like back before I say goodbye. A whole list of them in fact.'

There was just something about him that got up my nose, and from the stiff-lipped way he spoke I guessed he didn't like me either. He said nastily, 'If it was down to me you'd be banged up for the night.'

'Knickers,' I told him politely.

I won't repeat the word he said back but it would

112

probably make the average person blush. I was glad he'd said it quietly so the WPC over by the door didn't hear, she was definitely too young for such things. I thought I knew now why he hadn't made sergeant yet.

'You try it first,' I said, 'that way I'll pick up tips.' I hoped I never needed help from him in a hurry. Maybe I should give more practice to making friends and influencing people. He was a neat shade of crushed strawberry when I signed the receipt for my things, and he didn't say goodbye. I was really disappointed about that.

According to my newly restored watch it was four-thirty. Tom had either been hanging around my place for an hour, or he'd given up and gone home. Whichever way it was, another twenty minutes would be neither here nor there. I trotted to the locksmith's on Market Street and bought a Yale latch with a deadlock facility and a five lever mortice; anybody keen enough to get through those would have to be a real professional.

On the way to pick up a taxi I got in a few groceries. I had a feeling Tom's wife might not approve of the chocolate cream cake, what with all the calories and cholesterol, but if he'd been waiting that long he deserved a treat. And if he hadn't I could pick up a little comfort myself.

When I got out of the taxi on Palmer's Run there was a blue Volvo I hadn't seen before tucked in neatly at the kerb. I thought it was empty until I got level with it and saw Tom hunched down in the front seat. He looked like he'd gone to sleep. I tapped on the glass and he opened one eye and looked at me, then eased himself out onto the pavement.

'Been doing your shopping then?' he said. 'Or did they give you that lot down the police station?'

'Less of the sarcasm, I've had a bad day. I brought a reward for being patient.'

'I can see it through the bag. Temptation cake. Go on then, run up and get the kettle going.'

'Settle for a slow crawl,' I said. 'How did you know where I was?'

'Marcie on the second floor. Been telling me all about

the banging and thumping, said it sounded like they were doing a demolition job on you.'

'Looking for stolen goods.'

'Get on!' There was a definite lack of surprise, I squinted round at him.

'You knew about that too, didn't you?'

He tapped his nose. 'That's what makes certain things easier for me than you. I've got friends that let me know what's going on.'

I hit the top step and fished out my door keys. It must be useful to have police connections. I wondered why he'd quit the force, was it because he'd put in enough time to get a pension or because he'd been disillusioned? Not being the kind of person to stay in the dark when a smart question could turn the light on, I asked. The answer was fairly cryptic.

'Like you, love, I got tired of being squeezed both ends.' He didn't explain who'd been doing the squeezing and I let the question hang until later.

I opened up and made a beeline for the kitchen. 'Does Nicholls know about your pipeline?' I called back, filling the kettle. Silence; then a high-pitched squeal. I slammed in the plug and went to see what he was doing. He was shuffling round the hall with a little black box in his hand; the high-frequency squeal was coming from the box. Fascinating. He started poking around a pot plant.

I don't have room for a hall table, so I make do with a semi-circular rosewood piece fixed to the wall under a plain mirror. It suits me fine, but the bird's nest fern on top could do with some pruning and I trotted over to see why it had attracted Tom's attention.

His hand quit fiddling around the stalks and came out with a piece of micro-electronic wizardry. He closed it in the silence of his fist. 'You've been bugged,' he said like he was just telling me I'd won a prize. How nice. A sweep round the rest of the place turned up three more. It was getting beyond a joke.

'I hope you've got a clear conscience,' he said when he was through, 'because some joker's dead keen to find out

114

what you're up to; expensive toys like these don't get wasted collecting girl-talk.'

'Is that right?' I said angrily. I was sick of people tramping around all over my privacy. I didn't bother to ask his views on bug disposal, to my mind a hammer would suffice.

Tom's mind was of infinitely more evil bent, and as I burrowed through junk under the kitchen sink I could hear him messing with the radio until he came up with some heavy metal of his own. I hadn't thought Tom's musical taste would run to Motorhead but life is full of little surprises.

Things went quiet again. Maybe it wasn't his street after all.

Coming up from the cupboard a wave of sound hit me. 'Hey,' I yelled, 'enough is enough.' The cacophonic beat stopped. Hammer in hand I trotted into the living room and saw the bugs lined up on the radio.

'That, was wicked,' I said admiringly when he'd taken tissue out of his ears.

'Given somebody a bit of an earache,' he acknowledged. He turned the radio back on at a more comfortable level. 'Be interesting to know who's been infringing your civil liberties. Can't see it being a police job, there'd be too much red-tape to get through. I fancy you've had another visitor.'

'Several,' I agreed, and thought how I just love it when people treat my place like home from home – especially when I'm out. I wondered if maybe the next unfriendly move would be from bugs in the boudoir to a bomb in the bath, and it wasn't a relaxing thought to get to grips with. *Shit*, I was glad I'd led such a blameless life lately.

He got on the kind of look my father always wore the times I came in late, I guess some men are born to worry.

'You should think about getting your locks changed,' he said, as if I didn't already know it.

'It's in hand. I picked a couple up on my way home. What shall we do with these?' I looked at the bugs and hefted the hammer suggestively.

115

Tom said, 'If I was you I'd drop 'em in Nicholls' lap, give him something extra to worry about.'

'Maybe he dodged the red-tape, in which case he knows about them already.'

'Be an even bigger worry then, won't it? Threaten to let your MP know what he's been up to, that'd drop him right in it.'

He patted around his pockets. Tom wasn't a sharp dresser and his clothes had a tired look, the grey flannel pants hanging baggy on his seat and wrinkling up across the lap. Maybe the look came from carrying so much junk around. It amazes me the things men tote about on a just-in-case basis. Like empty tobacco tins. He shoved the bugs in and gave it a good rattle. 'Thought we were supposed to be having that chocolate cake,' he said. 'I'll starve to death waiting at this rate.'

That's something else I came to like about Tom, he always kept his mind on the important things, but right then I hadn't finished with my own worries. I wanted to know who'd been tuned into my wavelength, especially since finding an eavesdropper with an earache was likely to prove as rewarding as spotting a mugger with a truss. I made known my thoughts on the subject and he listened kindly to the idea that stuffing his face should come second to playing hunt the receiver.

When I'd finished he explained a few intricacies of micro-electronics that I hadn't known before. There was more to being a private investigator than I'd thought, like knowing how to tell the difference between bugs that trigger a voice operated tape mechanism on or very close to where they've been hidden, say a hundred feet or so maximum, and the type that relay to a regular receiver anything up to three miles distant. According to Tom I'd been infested with the second kind, and the jolly little aerial he'd found sharing the TV outlet in the window frame proved it.

I trotted off to put the kettle on, it's always wise to know when you're beaten.

116

CHAPTER TWENTY

WITH ONLY A mute plate to bear witness to where two chocoholics had pigged out, we got down to a serious exchange of news. Tom had been real busy, what with doing the things he got paid to do and fitting in some charity digging for me along the way. I was impressed. I was also envious that he had ways of operating I knew nothing about. It seemed that doors opened and tongues wagged wherever he turned up. Post-mortem findings? Yessir! No problem.

I thought about what Tom had just told me, putting myself back inside the art gallery the day Thorne died, with the rain stopped and people drifting away. There'd been a fine film of sweat on Thorne's skin when we came out into the foyer but I'd put it down to the muggy heat, now I guessed it wasn't that at all, and that maybe when he ducked into the Gents it had been for more than a pee. I marshalled up what little I knew about diabetics; it wasn't much.

Tom said, 'A lethal mix of procaine and adrenalin wouldn't have taken more than ten minutes, less than that even.'

I could forget about the Chinaman having ricin pellets in his umbrella, Thorne had murdered himself. I wondered who had tampered with the insulin bottle. I'd seen them around, small squat multi-dose bottles with rubber tops that allowed the right dose to be needled up. Only for Thorne it hadn't worked that way.

'Nice friends he had,' I said thoughtfully; 'it'd be interesting to know who was with him the night before.'

'He was away from his digs, so it could be he picked up a girl, or could be he spent it with someone he knew better

117

than that. Of course him not being a local seems to limit the field a bit, cut it down to someone he worked with.'

'Except he didn't seem all that popular.'

He looked at me as if I knew something he didn't, so I re-hashed the boy-talk I'd heard at the Three Tuns again; I thought I'd mentioned it before but I'd been over the same ground so many times now, it was hard to remember.

'Maybe I'll have a little word with Ken,' Tom said, 'seems a likely lad for trouble. This Probation Officer, Perryman. Someone you know personally, but how well?'

When you got right down to it the real answer to that was I didn't know much about Mike at all. I knew more about the milkman, and his three kids, and the wife who had a hard time with the second, and how he played darts Wednesday nights and took the family swimming on Sundays. Nice, friendly chit-chat that kept the world going round. But Mike? Damn it, I'd known the man four years and what I really knew about him was zilch. It gave me a guilty feeling as we picked over the few bones I had. When I dropped in Tony Murray's name as late night biker and Kawasaki owner, Tom guessed which road I was moving along.

'Wrong horse,' he said knowledgeably. 'Don't waste your money on it. It wasn't Murray put you in hospital.'

I love it when people blow holes in my theories.

'Right bike,' I pointed out, 'and right connections. He knew Mike, Mike knew Thorne, Thorne died in my lap.'

'Take my word, the Kawasaki wasn't Murray's. Somebody paid good money for your ambulance ride, enough to lose a licence for. And while we're on the subject think Robert Alan Lewis in place of Thorne.'

I guess I must have shown surprise because Tom got a 'see what a real detective can find out' look on his face. I didn't begrudge him, I know my limitations. He enlightened me some more. Lewis was an undercover Customs and Excise officer, working with Regional Crime, and the list of jobs he'd had dovetailed nicely with a bundle of art thefts. A couple of places, he was there when the job was done, the others he arrived a day or so after.

118

Blue Nude with Carnation swam into mind. Maybe it was true, maybe I didn't know a damn thing about art appreciation, maybe I'd seen Rembrandt's second coming and not recognised it. I pushed the idea around and found myself unworried. I pulled my mind back to what Tom was saying.

'. . . a couple of Corots, an early Picasso, two small Renoirs, that type of thing, easy to sell.'

'In a different league to the local art show, or was that a practice run?'

'No one is paying me to find out,' Tom said, 'not that you should take that as a complaint, because it isn't one, our arrangement stands, but my unbiased opinion now is that you should take Nicholls' advice and leave him to get on with it. My guess is, Lewis was getting closer than he knew, and if it was that easy to take him out it isn't a game for amateurs.'

I thought about that. It seemed to me that what I did from now on wasn't going to make any difference one way or the other, I was already fixed in someone's little mind as a nuisance. Hiding a pair of stolen paintings in the loft might not be in the same league as using me for hedgehog practice, but it wasn't the kind of trick you'd play on a friend. I shared my thoughts with Tom but he wasn't impressed.

'Keep swimming where the sharks are,' he said, 'and the water's likely to redden up a bit. Thanks for the chocolate cake, we'll have to do it again some time.'

I said, 'There's something else you know, isn't there, something you're not going to tell me?'

He spread his hands, his face as innocent as Ron's had been when he told me he hadn't a Sunday market. 'Can't think where you got that idea. Going to let Nicholls have the bugs?'

'Why don't you drop them in for me.'

'Going for maximum annoyance?' he said equably. 'I'll drop 'em in on the way home if you like, but don't be surprised if you get a visit.'

'With luck I'll have changed the locks by then,' I said.

119

He grinned. 'Don't know why we worry about you.'
'Don't think I'm not grateful.'

I walked with him to the door and watched him go down the steps, when he got to the bend he called back. 'Take care.'

'You bet,' I said, and tried to remember where I'd put the screwdriver.

Like a lot of supposedly all male jobs, when you got right down to it changing locks wasn't all that difficult, and Saturday night I slept securely. Of course anybody with SAS training could have swung in through the window, but somehow that didn't bother me much. When I woke next day the weather had hotted up again, and the sky was that shade of cerulean artists break into a sweat over.

I thought how good it would feel to do a couple of circuits in the park. Limbering up didn't cause me any problems, so I pulled on a pair of cut-offs and a navy sweat top and set off at an easy pace. I'd slept late, which seemed to prove I had a guilt-free conscience, and it was already a little after nine. When I came level with Dora's I slowed right down and admired the neat rows of bricks where the new garage was going up.

It entered my head that the little matter of who was doing what to whom needed sorting out before I got invited to park anything else in there.

A replay might not leave Dora so lucky. I wished that idea hadn't got into my mind, I didn't want it to be my fault if Dora got hurt, I was really fond of her. Logic came and said if I didn't garage there, she was safe. I hoped logic was right for once.

I trotted on; all I needed was to make the pieces fit.

Some people are born optimistic, others catch it when the weather's nice.

I made it to the park and did a circuit before my legs decided the grass looked too good to waste. I headed for a sunny patch and looked around for doggie-doos.

With a few exceptions dogs are nice creatures and I don't go along with the anti-dog brigade, by and large

120

dogs do what humans teach them to do, and from what I see around Bramfield half the dog-owners must crap on their living-room carpets.

I flopped and started kneading where my calf muscles had bunched up; so what if some people ran on through the pain barrier? I was made of more fragile stuff.

From where I'd hunkered down I could watch the state of play on the tennis courts; four out of the six were busy and I guessed the other two would be before long. The tennis might not be great but the outfits made up for it; I hadn't realised they were making shorts that small, maybe I was starting to get old. I watched a redhead retrieve a ball and winced it looked so painful, but then again, maybe she liked being sliced in two. The two heroes on the next court seemed to be having a few concentration problems, but that didn't surprise me either, it wasn't the kind of thing their mothers would have thought to warn them about.

I shifted my position so I could watch a mixed doubles. They were playing well, but that wasn't what I found interesting; instead, it was the girl in the bright yellow overalls sitting on a bench with her back to the high chain-link fencing. She'd brought her knitting with her; something small and white, and I thought maybe it wouldn't hurt to go and talk to her, I was curious to know how the protest at the multi-storey was making out. I trotted diagonally across the grass and let myself in quietly through the metal gate. When she realised I wasn't a stranger butting in she moved down the seat a little and I dropped down beside her.

'Thought it was you,' I said cheerfully. 'How's the picketing coming along, any more old Viking coins turn up?'

'Would you believe a bit of bronze helmet?'

'Just lying around?'

'Well no, they dig these big pits you know and fill them with hard-core and poured concrete. Most of them are filled in already but there's one or two on the far side they haven't got around to yet.'

'No accounting for luck.'

121

'So right.'

The smiley-looking male across the other side of the net gave her a wave and she gave him one back. 'I'd be over there with him, if it wasn't for Sprog,' she sighed, and gave her bulge a pat. 'Roll on July.'

'First one?'

'Second. Grandma's got Harriet for the morning. She's three. I tried bringing her once but she kept trotting off with the balls.'

'Dangerous too,' I said as a ball bent the fence a little to my right.

'She has to learn to duck sometime,' she said philosophically. 'I'm Jenny Mace, by the way.'

'Leah Hunter.' We gave each other a little handshake. 'So what happened when the bronze turned up?'

She grinned. 'There's a temporary injunction on building. It won't last long but it'll give the MP time to get something done with the Environment Minister.'

'Mmm, mmm, that's going to upset the council again.'

'Not just them,' she said confidingly. 'I've heard the famous Mr Denton has his finger in the pie.'

'Is that right?' The idea burrowed into my mind and raised a few hares. Denton was connecting in with a lot of things besides tax evasion.

'That's what I've heard,' Jenny said. 'I know somebody put up money, and who else has that kind of finance around here?'

'I thought it was a council project.'

'So did we until a leak came from someone who knew someone, who knew someone – you know the way it goes.'

'It must be in the council minutes somewhere, it's the kind of thing they'd need central government permission for.'

She gave me a sharp look. 'You're not just the average citizen, are you?' she said, 'not if you know about that kind of thing.' I could tell she was wondering if I was a sneaky kind of council spy and she'd said too much already. I put my hands up.

'HM Taxes,' I said, 'and we always like to know who's making money without telling us. Don't worry, I'm not going to go running to tell what you're up to. On a purely personal level I'm on your side.' She looked relieved.

'Sometimes I talk too much,' she admitted. 'I put it down to hormones, I'm not half so chatty when I'm not pregnant.'

'I haven't been there myself. Maybe one day.'

'When the right man comes along?'

'Something like that. Close relationships don't appeal right now, I work on a once bitten twice shy basis. Maybe when I get to feel maternal I'll join a sperm bank.'

'Ouch, that sounds like something really hurt.' She put down her knitting and gave me one of those sympathetic looks women are supposed to be good at. 'Want to talk about it?'

It had been three years and I hadn't talked about it to anyone, I guessed I could handle it alone for a little longer. Anyway it wasn't the kind of thing a woman in her condition wanted to hear; right then she had one and seven-ninths children and a good-looking husband – she didn't want to know that smiley over there might go looking for a little extra.

'Thanks,' I said, 'but it's one of those things best left buried.' I watched the game a couple of minutes and decided it was time to go. I got up and did all the nice social things and genuinely hoped we'd meet up again.

I trotted back to the path and headed for home, when I got to the bend and looked back the game had ended and Jenny and smiley had their heads together. Nice.

I wished I hadn't been made to think about Will again, when things hurt that much they get buried deep, and I'd got along with my life very well since I trashed his toothbrush; no need to freeze just because one fire got out of hand.

The real hurt came from Will not having had guts

enough to tell me he was married, it isn't the kind of thing to hear second-hand. I guess he knew that if he'd been honest right along I wouldn't have let him play in my backyard. I pushed my legs harder, glad they hurt. Damn it, I'd really loved the rat!

CHAPTER TWENTY-ONE

IT WAS HARD to decide which was more unlovely, the rubble littered waste, or the half-dozen rows of back-to-backs still standing. Personally I plumped for the rubble, entropy is always ugly. Something large, dark and furry scuttled from one boarded-up house to another and I cursed Charlie for getting it wrong; nobody lived around here any more, the grime ridden houses were corpses waiting for a man with a shovel.

The hybrid lurched from one pothole to the next, the grass-fringed cobbles strewn with half-bricks and broken glass, maybe I should get on to Charlie for a new set of tyres.

The last row was Grundy Street.

Number five still had a lace curtain halfway up its window, so did its neighbour; it was hard to tell what colour they'd been to begin with because they'd lapsed to an overall grey colour. I sat outside and wondered whether to bother, what did I need picklocks for? The curtain took on a darker grey; *this is the watchdog watching the watchdog, this is the watchdog watching you.* I revved the engine gently and debated with myself. Did I have reason to distrust Charlie? No. So what was worrying me? Number five's door opened before I got round to answering that, and I got another of life's surprises.

Sid didn't belong in that kind of house, his Pringle sweater and hand-made shoes said so. I guessed he'd be pushing sixty and he looked the kind of man it'd be safe to buy insurance from. That worried me, no one who knew Charlie and sold picklocks should look that honest. He gave me a friendly smile and showed off his good teeth. I wound down the window. 'Sid?'

'Come on in,' he said, 'there's nothing in here that bites.'
I was glad to hear that, but I wondered how he could be
so sure. I got out and locked up.

'It must get lonely around here,' I said, 'now everyone
else is gone.'

He smiled a bit more and went back inside, leaving the
door uninvitingly open. When I followed on the air that
came out to meet me smelled musty. The door opened
right into the living room, and I guessed that must have
been a really fun arrangement in winter. I say 'have been'
because it was obvious as soon as I got in that no one lived
there any more.

'School,' said Sid with a flick of his hand, 'never was as
fancy as home.'

I didn't know which school he'd been to, but if where we
were now was anything to go by, Dotheboy's Hall would
have had a waiting list; underfoot the lino was shredding
itself, and a three-legged table had a pile of bricks propping
up its fourth corner. Apart from grey mould curtains on
the walls and a cardboard box at his feet, that was it as far
as furnishings went.

'Nice,' I said. 'What's the rent like?'

He grinned. 'Peppercorn. Charlie give you a price?'

'No.'

'Wicked man. Not the sort of thing you'd find in
Woolies.'

'Everything goes on profit margins these days.'

'Capitalism at its worst. A hundred and fifty and I'm
doing you a favour.' He set the box on the table and it
rocked a little with the weight.

The little zipped case he gave me felt soft and supple
and looked like a manicure set. 'Best Moroccan leather,' he
said. 'Ladies' special, don't get much call for them, funnily
enough.'

'Boots do better value.' I opened it up. The tools
were slim and shiny and covetable, they reminded me
of Meccano sets that were strictly for the boys.

'Course if you're not serious there's no obligation, I owe
Charlie a favour or two.'

126

'A hundred,' I said.

'One thirty.'

'A hundred.'

'One twenty-five.'

'A hundred.'

'You'll do well,' Sid said. 'Charlie didn't mention what line you were in.'

'Funny,' I said, 'he didn't tell me much about you either. It'll have to be a cheque.'

'Don't go much for cheques. Let Charlie have the cash tomorrow and I'll pick it up from him.' I offered the case back but he didn't take it. 'Trust,' he said, 'that's what life's all about. Consider this, if you don't pay up I'll have it off Charlie: one way or another.' He was still smiling but I had a feeling that about now was the time to read the small print.

'Nice man, Charlie,' I said.

'Looks after his friends,' Sid agreed. 'Now how about me showing you how to play with your new toys?'

I'd been wondering what else he had in the box. The answer was locks – big, small, ancient, modern; obviously there was a dedicated collector here.

I picked up a five lever mortice and unzipped my little case again; now was as good a time as any to find out if my attic nest was as secure as I hoped.

I wasn't sure if I'd struck a good bargain for the tool set, I wasn't even sure why I wanted it, but I was a lot more knowledgeable about locks when I left Sid than I had been before we met. If Thomas Magnum ever needed a partner, I was the girl. I daydreamed a bit, especially about the side benefits. Like the man said, we are such stuff as dreams are made on. I almost jumped a red light and the flutter brought me back to earth. The last thing I needed was another insurance claim. I waited for the lights to change. A black Kawasaki went by on the main road just as amber joined the red. I flicked the indicator from right to left and got a hoot from a Sierra lined up behind as I swung the wheel. He didn't know I was celebrating road-hog day.

Every town has its no-go area: no-go for some people, that is, for others it's as natural a place to be as under a stone. Bramfield's seedy zone edged onto the dereliction around Grundy Street, and I'd picked up a few tit-bits about it from Sid while we'd been playing with locks. Denton really shouldn't try to hide away his assets the way he did, but I was going to have fun talking to his accountant when I got back to work.

The Kawasaki rider wasn't bothering to pick up speed so I guessed he would be stopping soon, and I kept a couple of cars between us. Most of the crumbling buildings that lined the road had been scheduled for demolition for years, but for some reason a reprieve kept coming through. According to Sid, Denton had a lot to do with that. If the red-light area got cleaned up he'd lose a lot of money. His name wasn't on the sex shop's painted-up windows, and the prostitutes who weren't free-lancing didn't walk around carrying rent-a-fuck cards with his number on, but as Sid said, these things get known. The Kawasaki stopped and I turned into a side-street almost opposite and braked. Through the back window I watched the helmet come off.

Bingo!

I wondered what Tony Murray wanted with a sex shop – business or pleasure. It grieved me not to be able to find out. I turned the car and settled down to wait; while I waited I tried out a new equation. It went Lewis, alias Thorne + Perryman + Murray + Denton, and it had to add up to a very complicated answer.

Fifteen minutes later Murray came out and put on his helmet, I started the hybrid up. At that time on a Sunday there wasn't much traffic, and there was only a Montego between us. Half a mile along, the Montego turned off and there was just Murray and me. Down near the lake where the monied citizens lived the Kawasaki swung off the road onto a curving drive. I went on by and headed for home.

Behind me Denton and Murray obviously had something to talk about, and I'd have given a whole lot to know what it was.

CHAPTER TWENTY-TWO

DENTON'S BUSINESS INTERESTS encompassed a diverse range of activities, and Murray could be just one more employee on his payroll. The way jobs were these days, a lot of people had to grab whatever was on offer, and I didn't think Murray could afford to be too choosy, especially if he still had the habit. With heroin selling on the street at around seventy-five pounds a gram, and cocaine not much cheaper, he wouldn't mind too much what he had to do to earn the kind of money it took to buy the stuff. And then there was the Kawasaki – top of range and flashy; Murray must have real money worries. I slowed right down while I thought about that. He had to be getting a lot of cash from somewhere.

I needed somebody to talk to who knew about these things. Mike would have been a help, no one knew what was going down on the dark side of Bramfield as well as he did, and maybe that was why he wasn't around any more.

I'd have given a lot to get into Tony Murray's bedsit and look around while he wasn't there, but I knew it wasn't a practical idea. I cruised slowly in the light traffic. I had that wound-up kind of feeling that comes when you get a mind full of problems and there aren't any answers around.

After a while I knew I needed some company. Most times I like being alone but right then I wanted friendly voices. Male company would have been extra nice, but at that point in my life there wasn't anyone I wanted to get that close to; not unless you counted Nicholls. I accepted there were still some interesting possibilities there but it would take time.

I headed for Em's and a little fussing; family life is nice in small doses, especially when things aren't going too good in other areas.

It was around ten when I got home and patted the hybrid goodnight. I put some milk on low heat and took a quick shower while it warmed up; there's nothing to beat a combination of cocoa and TV for inducing sleep. Isn't it a shit the way things never work out the way you plan?

I plumped a few cushions and settled down nice and comfy. About the time in my life when I'd been hooked on Bananarama, my mother had this urge to glue herself to anything that had James Garner in it, and right then the *Rockford Files* were having a re-re-re-run. Considering how little my mother and I have in common, watching it seemed a nice way to achieve an overdue bonding. I gave the storyline more than my usual attention in case I could pick up a few tips.

It was the first time I'd noticed how often Rockford got beaten up through no fault of his own, it seemed all he had to do to be in trouble was open his caravan door. I began to feel a certain empathy with him.

I also felt envy.

The getting in trouble part was easy, I was really good at that, but I just didn't have his flair for finding out why.

The other thing that inched into my brain was the way unauthorised entry netted him good results; it put me in mind of the neat leather case full of shiny bits of metal that I'd got from Sid. Charlie had been right to wonder why a tax inspector wanted picklocks, I'd been wondering about it myself until right that minute when the answer crawled out of my subconscious. I tried to damp down the urge to go out and do some illicit sleuthing, especially since real life has a habit of ignoring fictional rules. The problem is I've always found it hard to take good advice, even when it's my own, and tonight was no different.

I left Rockford to get on with rounding up the bad guys while I worried about how easy it was to drop into bad habits. I also worried about getting caught. Pleading good intentions wouldn't be likely to cut much ice.

The debate with myself was fierce. My job helped prop

up the Establishment, damn it; I wasn't supposed to change sides. *But,* came back that part of my nature Gran always said would get me in real trouble one day: I wouldn't be changing sides, it would only look that way to the unimaginative.

Like Nicholls, or a judge and jury.

Self-righteousness crept in. Had I *asked* to be involved? I had not. I'd been dragged in willy-nilly, and that gave me a perfect right to find out why.

Except I was supposed to be one of the watchdogs; get caught on the wrong side of the fence and someone would take away my bone.

As a deterrent argument that didn't work. To begin with it smacked of injustice, what mattered was why the poor dog was out there, and I knew nobody would ask.

I gave up, sometimes arguments can't be won. Around midnight I dressed up in a black sweat-suit and soft-shoed it downstairs and out onto the street. I didn't put on the hybrid's lights until I got past Dora's, and when I reached Burntwood Drive I turned them off again and parked at the top of the gradient, where an over-hanging tree blocked off the street-light a few doors up from Mike's house.

I gave his loose gravel drive a miss, keeping to the grass edging and round to the back door. Like his neighbours Mike went in for high fencing and good thick shrubs, and I didn't have to worry about my little torch being noticed when I got to work on the lock. It's amazing how much knowledge you can pick up in one afternoon. I got a real kick out of hearing the levers click back.

Another little pearl of knowledge Sid had imparted was the way nine out of ten domestic alarm systems have a pad just inside the door to set them off; I took good care not to step on the Welcome mat. Like Gran used to say, two minutes' thought saves ten minutes' tears.

It's disheartening to be somewhere and not know why; I really wished I knew what I was looking for. I got tired of the kitchen and moved into the front room. The curtains were wide open and orange tinted moonlight gave the furniture a surrealist hue. It seemed like a good idea to

131

close them. I was halfway to the window when the sound froze me: anyone with a front door key had to have a better right than me to be there.

Sh-it!

I eased a leather settee gently out from the wall and crawled into the gap. The front door closed quietly but no lights went on. Interesting.

Someone walked in from the hall and the connecting door closed; there was a swish of sound from the curtains as whoever it was stole my idea. Maybe it was Mike back from wherever he'd been. It was a good thought; better than a concrete grave. I sweated in the narrow space and worried about useful excuses, then the light went on and I stopped worrying about that and started on something new, like what was Tony Murray doing there, black leathers and all.

I couldn't see a damn thing from where I was except the door and the light switch, but I could hear him moving furniture around, grunting with the effort of it. I eased along to get a peek. He'd shifted out a Victorian bookcase and rolled back the carpet; that way he could get at a neat little hidey-hole underneath.

I got a nice warm feeling thinking how Nicholls' buddies had missed out when they searched this place, maybe they only found things when they were told where to look. When he started shoving the furniture back it seemed like a good time to sneak out and let him have the place to himself. I reached up and eased gently on the door knob, balanced low, ready to move fast. A breath of air moved in and Tony turned his head, for a couple of seconds we stared at each other. The pink edges round his eyes said he was still a user and I guessed that right then what he wanted most was a fix. He had a very mean look on his face as he halved the distance between us.

Since it didn't seem like a good time to start a conversation I came up off my toes and made it out into the hall in quick time, then I worried about which of us could move the faster.

132

I headed for the back door and Tony came too, wasting breath on names a gentleman would never think of using.

The sprint through the kitchen was the fastest I'd ever made, and I really blessed the careless way I hadn't locked up behind me when I came in.

I kept the same speed going until I reached the hybrid, behind me all hell had broken loose. It was a real shame I'd stepped on the mat coming out.

The electric bell sounded deafening against the silent night, and I had a feeling Murray would forget about coming after me in his hurry to get away.

Adrenalin was still pumping round my system and I felt good; like Rockford I'd got some of what I was after and I was on a high, taking in deep breaths of oxygen and laughing with the sheer primitive pleasure of success.

Lights were going on in houses and I guessed somebody would be ringing the police. I hunched down in the car and waited; no sense in drawing attention to my being there. A minute or so later I heard Murray's Kawasaki roar into life – I was glad about that, it would give the neighbours something to tell the fuzz about.

I gave it a couple of minutes longer then eased off the handbrake and let the car roll gently down the gradient; just before the bottom I started up the engine and drove sedately away. The high was wearing off and by tomorrow I'd be stuck with a conscience waiting for Nicholls to show up, but tomorrow could take care of itself, right now I was taking home new pieces of puzzle and working out the odds on them fitting in.

CHAPTER TWENTY-THREE

I DIDN'T SLEEP all that well, but it wasn't conscience that kept me awake, it was fitting in the new pieces of jigsaw. I could see the beginnings of a picture, and I'd have been well satisfied if it wasn't for one thing: no matter how I turned it around I ended up with Mike on the wrong side. That stash under his floorboards couldn't have been there without his knowledge.

It was hard to handle the idea of Mike and Murray working together, selling quick trips to wonderland, getting rich out of bad habits, but I didn't think the polythene packet I'd seen Murray with had held cooking salt.

Customs and Excise spent the biggest part of its budget trying to stop drugs getting onto the market, picking up new trafficking routes and sealing them off. Sometimes they did more, sometimes they followed the route in, tracking back to where the money to pay for it came from. I remembered how the gravel had hurt my knees at the art gallery, and how Thorne, or Lewis, or whoever, hadn't deserved to die the way he did.

Finally my brain tired itself out and I slept for around four hours before it woke up and got hooked into the puzzle again. By then a lot of things had sorted themselves out, and I could see why a little innocent snooping had been so upsetting. I must have been a real pain in the ass, especially when I didn't react the way they expected and cry all the way home to Mama's house.

There were still missing pieces I had to find, like why two rubbish paintings held so much importance, and where the big money was coming from – not Mike or Murray, I was sure of that. The dog I gave a bad name was Denton. Maybe I only had one villain on my back, after all.

I took a shower and made myself neat and tidy, the way one has to be to do any snooping in official places, then I ate a good breakfast in case I didn't have time to get around to food again for a while.

I swung into HM Taxes like I had every right to be there. What's a little sick leave between friends? Pete doesn't miss much. I'd no chance of sneaking into the file room with his beady little eyes watching me go by. I fixed an innocent smile as he came out through his office door.

'You're looking well, Leah.' His eyes travelled the snaky pink scar. 'Must have hurt. Poor old you.'

'I'm over it, the best bruises are out of sight.'

'Interesting. Come show me the full horror and I'll offer tea and sympathy.'

No one I ever met could leer in quite the same way as Pete; one day I'd pick up on him and watch him wriggle. His hand on my shoulder had the familiarity of long practice, and I trotted meekly into his office, time enough to slap him down when I'd got what I wanted.

He stuck his head back out and told Cathy to round up some tea; being office junior doesn't change much, it's still a pain. I sat in the visitor's chair and tried to look artless, something I always find hard. Pete came back and parked his bum. His swivel chair tilts back a bit so he can put his feet on the desk; he did that now, lacing his hands over his head.

'Why do I get the feeling this is less a courtesy call than a way of underhand infiltration?' he said. 'From memory there's another week on your sick note, you should be in Marbella recovering.'

'Too much lust and cheap wine wouldn't be good for me right now,' I told him. 'Anyway, I need to check some figures in the Denton file; the case is up in court again the day I get back, and I wouldn't want to get caught out by a smart lawyer.'

That's something else I'd learned when I was small: half-truths can get you off the hook better than whole lies. Pete knew Denton would be in court again, and I

135

did want to check some figures; he wasn't to know the two things were unconnected.

'That'll be the day,' Pete said acidly.

'Oh, come on, Pete, I do still work here, you know.' He gave me a hawky look and it worried me. So did what he said next.

'I've um . . . sent your name forward for a high-flying admin course that week, thought you'd like it, time you moved up, stretched your wings.'

'I'd get vertigo and I like what I'm doing now, thanks all the same.'

'It's residential,' he said. 'Malvern. Nice little place. Healthy.'

'Send Arnold.'

'Arnold'll be in court, you'll be in Malvern,' he told me flatly. 'Forget about Denton.'

I took what he said on board and didn't like it; I felt he'd been got at, but I wasn't going to argue the point right then. 'So let Arnold tangle with the next Kawasaki,' I said off-handedly, 'but I'll still need to take a look in Denton's file. I'd just hate for Arnold to go to court with the wrong information, and so would you.'

That's the only guaranteed way to win an argument with Pete, hoist him on to his efficiency petard. Cathy came in carrying a couple of mugs with tea-bag pulls hanging out over the side: I hate that. Pete patted her hip. 'One more little errand, Catherine, my love. Fetch the Denton file up, it'll be in the current prosecution slot.'

I felt unfriendly; the way I saw it the male half of society took a whole lot too much for granted. I decided a grumble wouldn't be unreasonable after all.

'Pete,' I said, 'for the record I don't want to move up, down, or sideways right now, and Arnold could make a mess of it, he isn't familiar with Denton's case.'

Pete tut-tutted and his fingers twitched on the blotter. So help me, if he patted my knee he'd be sorry. 'Give him a week and he will be,' he said reasonably, and added a sweetener. 'Leah, dear, you're very good at your job,

136

that's why it might be time to move on to better things. Trust me, I'm your boss.'

I said nastily, 'I take it Nicholls has been complaining again. What is it this time?'

I'd hit the button. Pete said uneasily, 'Nothing, except how much better off you'd be occupied elsewhere for a while.'

He dunked the tea-bag up and down; it's amazing how little things please little minds that don't want to look you in the eye.

I said, 'Pete, I feel I could have a relapse. It'd be a shame to waste all that money on a course I might miss.' That stopped him playing. One thing HM auditors don't like is empty chairs; I could see him working out whether he could get Arnold over there if I stayed home.

He set the mug in the middle of his blotter and sat up straight; I knew the signs. Pete was going to be the heavy boss. Actually it's something he's quite good at, mainly because it's so unnerving having an amiable, hung-over loser turn into a sharp-edged exec.

Of course it didn't work so well on me, I've known him a long time. He said carefully, 'It would be short-sighted to put back promotion prospects over a personal difference. I have to point that out to you, Leah, just so there's no misunderstanding.'

'None at all,' I agreed. 'I just hope I stay healthy, you know how it would break my heart to let you down.' Cathy came in right then with a fat file. I got up and took it from her before she got inside Pete's reach.

Pete said stiffly, 'Bring it back to me when you're through.'

Like I said, he can really chill out when he wants to.

I sat at my own little desk and people wandered up and were nice to me. In between times I went through Denton's assets. There was nothing about the multi-storey site, but a good accountant would get out of that by saying it came into next year's returns. What couldn't be got out of was income from the property on Pontefract Road. If I believed Sid, Denton had shaken out every other

137

property owner along the sleazy mile or so some time back. Which meant the takings from the members-only cinema club, the dirty-mac revue bar, and the collars-up sex shop, were all his.

I got a glow out of thinking what fun I'd have checking it all out.

Pete was still in a mood when I took the file back in. I poured a little oil. 'Thanks, Pete, I really appreciate you letting me check things out. I haven't made any amendments, everything seems all right, nothing to stop the case going along smoothly.' I could see him relax at that, but he wasn't going to let me know about it.

'That's good,' he said, leafing through the file without looking at me. 'Any more worries pass them on to either me or Arnold. Give me a ring Friday and I'll let you know the final arrangements for Monday.'

That's another thing about Pete in a mood; he doesn't let go easily.

Having council departments in the same building was really convenient; for the first time I saw an advantage in their moving out of the Town Hall, for one thing it saved me having to find somewhere else to park. I took the lift up to the top floor and then wished I hadn't, it's the kind that staggers from side to side and leaves you wondering if the string is going to hold.

The Planning Department was a hive of activity. The whole place was open plan, so nobody felt put upon by not having an office as nice as the snot down the corridor who never did any work and got paid twice as much.

I trotted around in ever-increasing circles until I found the right desk. It struck me that maybe things weren't quite so equal after all; if they had been most of the females wouldn't be relegated to one corner pecking at keyboards. It made me glad I'd worn my business suit that day; that's another thing I've learned about male dominated areas – if you don't want chatting up or patting up you have to look efficient.

There was a white plastic block on the desk that had 'Denis Higgs' stamped on in black letters; I supposed it

138

would be necessary in that size of office, or it would be easy to forget who you were.

Higgs looked weary and so did his clothes, everything about him sagged downwards, but the look improved when he was on his feet and heading out of the office; I had to trot to keep up with him. We ended up in a room full of box files, grey cabinets, and chests with large shallow drawers. It didn't take him long to come up with the details I wanted about the Pontefract Road properties; Denton's name wasn't mentioned directly but there are ways of getting around that, and I knew Northern Properties Ltd was just a bit of camouflage, peel it back and Denton would be sitting in the middle of it.

Without being asked, he took the planning applications over to the photocopier and ran off some copies. I said, 'Thanks, that's just what I needed. Do you mind looking something else up?'

'Gets me out of the deep litter for a while longer,' he said; 'anything that does that has to be worthwhile. What is it you want?'

'I'd be interested to know if there's just council money financing the new multi-storey car park.'

He moved to another cabinet. 'Heard about the protest committee?'

'I've seen the pickets out.'

'Can't blame them, could have used the land for something better.'

'Didn't anybody say so?'

'Paid officers offer advice, it's up to the planning committee if they take it or not.'

'But they didn't in this case?'

'No, the feedback was we were being over-cautious. Of course the arguments for a car park were cogent enough, the town needs more off-street parking and wherever you sited a multi-storey there'd be complaints; happens every time. When it's up and running it'll all die down.' He shuffled his fingers through the files. 'As far as finance goes I can tell you without looking it isn't all council money, which probably made a difference to the way they looked at things, especially with a share of profits going into the council budget. It's the old gift-horse story.' He opened up a file and let me read it. The original application had been back to committee three times before it got through.

I said, 'It looks like some people were hard to convince. I wonder what changed their minds?'

His shrug was expressive. 'Rumour was, a lot of the opposition stayed home that night.'

I flipped pages and found the council's building partners listed as Bramfield City and County Development Company Ltd. Nice name, I thought, a really solid and dependable sound to it. I wondered if Denton employed someone to think them up.

'All I need now is a list of directors.'

'Can't help you there, it wouldn't be something planning needed to know, except . . .' He took the file and turned back a few pages. 'There – original application, registered office Grayson & Chubb, 18 Park Square, Bramfield.' I scribbled it on the back of a photocopy.

'What about this other one – Redwood Properties Ltd? Have you got the registered address for them?'

'Might have.' He took a box file down and sorted through the pink sheets inside. 'Here we are. G. W. Bentham, Accountants, Millhill.'

'Thanks,' I said, 'I know them well, and I appreciate your help.'

'A pleasure.' He added cryptically, 'I don't know what it is you're looking for but mind where you put your feet, there's a lot of egg-shells around.'

It was one of the things I gave some thought to on the way to see Denton's accountant. Bentham's offices were over a stationer's supply shop on a quiet back street. I'd been up the narrow flight of stairs many times before, and the typist cum receptionist cum switchboard operator cum tea-lady knew me well. I can't say she ever looked pleased to see me, and I guessed some of that had rubbed off from Bentham. He was always polite, usually helpful with anything that wouldn't weigh against him or a client, but I always had the feeling he'd rather do business with a

140

horse than a woman. That didn't bother me much, it was his problem.

Bentham kept me waiting a while so I'd know my place in the scheme of things and then buzzed me through, heaving himself half out of his chair when I went in, no mean task considering the size of him. I settled on the spindle-back visitor's chair and waited until he'd got his chins comfy again.

He said, 'I heard you were having some sick leave, it's nice you've recovered so fast.'

The first time I'd heard him speak his voice had thrown me. Like a *castrato* grown old, his voice was too high for the size of him.

I said, 'It's nice of you to be concerned. I came to talk about Redwood Properties Ltd, it is one of Denton's companies, isn't it?'

He steepled his fingers and thought about that. You'd expect a fat man to have podgy hands, but his were dainty compared to the rest of him, so, come to that, were his feet. After a bit he said, 'Obviously that's a detail you know already. Is there a tax problem with that particular company?'

'Yes, I think you could say that, it doesn't seem to be shown on any tax returns made on Denton's behalf. I'd be interested to know why.'

'So would I, my dear child, so would I,' he said earnestly. 'And it's something I shall look into immediately, I promise you. I can only suggest an administrative error; a typist turning over two pages; careless, but it happens.'

'Unoriginal but possible. Redwood Properties owns the half mile fronting the Pontefract Road, I believe. The red-light bit where the dirty macs and kerb crawlers hang out.'

He said, 'I don't think the area is as black as you paint it, Miss Hunter, and in any case my client can hardly be held responsible for street traffic of any kind.'

'Well now, I could argue about that,' I said. 'I hear he gets a cut of takings from the girls working that area.'

He stopped steepling and began a tattoo.

141

'That's a suggestion Mr Denton might find actionable.'

'Only if untrue, otherwise it's still counted taxable income,' I pointed out. 'Perhaps you haven't fully advised Mr Denton on that. We're back in court on Monday, I believe, I'd hate for there to be more charges.'

He said coldly, 'I'll find out what happened to the returns and let you have the full picture before Monday.'

'Yes, do that,' I said, 'and maybe you might remember a few other things too, like the Bramfield City and County Development Company.'

This time I'd surprised him, there wasn't any way to mistake that. Maybe Denton didn't tell him everything, after all.

'It is another of Denton's companies, isn't it?' I pushed. 'With a very large turnover, from what I hear, and no tax returns put in for that either. You've been very lax, Mr Bentham.'

I'd hit a sore spot there and his face puced up nicely. For a second or two I worried about him, then he got his voice back and said shirtily, 'That particular company is not among my client's holdings, Miss Hunter. For once your information source has seriously misled you, but as for the other matter I'll put it in hand immediately. Right now, if you don't mind, I have other business.' He shuffled a few papers around and looked at his desk.

I got up to go.

'I'm through now anyway,' I said. 'I'll get a list of directors for Bramfield City and County and let you have a copy if it turns out to be relevant.'

'Do that,' he came back huffily.

There's one part of my nature that can be really sneaky, and while I have to admit it might not be the most desirable character trait it's certainly one of the most useful. I sat in the hybrid and waited for Pete to go out for lunch. At exactly one he made the short trip from the back door to the XR3i that was his current sex aid. I hid behind a copy of the *Telegraph* and caught the black gleam as he went by; after a couple of minutes I locked up and went into the building.

142

There's no sense in looking guilty if you're doing something wrong. It annoyed me that I should need to sneak around when I worked in the damn place. I trotted into the file room and started hunting the Redwood Properties file. The big question on my mind was corporate taxes; if they weren't being paid Denton was in a heap more trouble. I located the binder and saw that this time Bentham had been good; he'd filed returns. I added a little note to say a good comb through might be profitable, and put the file back in place. For the time being that had to be someone else's headache.

Then I moved over to the B section and looked for Bramfield City and County. This time I was out of luck, no such file existed. I supposed I couldn't expect everything to drop into my lap nice and easy. I'd just have to visit Messrs Grayson & Chubb and bend a few more ears.

CHAPTER TWENTY-FOUR

I HAD A feeling Nicholls might be looking for me, which seemed as good a reason as any for not putting myself where he might think to look. I ran through all the places that might be, and came up with the greasy café near Probation as the safest spot to eat. The memory of frying potato hit my stomach and it rolled in fond remembrance; never mind the polystyrene, get with the chip butties. It's terrible how junk food exerts this irresistible pull when I'm feeling stressed. I parked in the alley behind the café and hoped nothing bigger than a Fordson wanted to get by.

Being so close to Probation means the two places tend to share clientele; that didn't bother me too much, five years in Bramfield Girls' Academy had failed to produce the effect desired by my parents. Unlike Em I hadn't come out the other end refined into a young lady. I looked around for the table with the least debris and settled down to eat, the lunch-time rush had gone and there were only two more tables taken. Over by the window two pubescent girls were showing a lot of leg in a way I didn't think their mothers would approve, and at the other two spotty youths were having a good look. The giggles and eye-corner glances seemed to be working, and I wondered if the two Lolitas knew what they might be getting themselves into.

On the next table somebody had left a copy of the *Sun* and I propped it up against the vinegar bottle and caught up on the day's news. 'MP's Cami-Knicker Cavortings' pushed insignificant things like recession and Balkan riots right out of my mind. When the door opened and let in another customer I didn't look up, I was too engrossed in things one could do with an ostrich feather.

144

After a bit I put the paper back with the other trash and checked up on the come-hither girls. They'd increased their audience by one, but I have to admit Tony Murray didn't look all that impressed. I was glad about that. I hid behind the *Sun* again and kept a sneaky eye on things round the edge.

After a couple of minutes Murray went out and the two youths got up and followed him, whatever interest they'd had in the girls, gone. I picked up my coffee and went around the front of the counter.

Outside the greasy window Tony straddled his Kawasaki like a TV sex symbol, all done up in black leather and silver studs. If somebody hadn't been a butterfingers I'd have thought the acne-necks were admiring the bike, but I saw the fast way the little white packet got picked up and pushed into a jeans pocket.

Any doubts I had left about Murray disappeared right then. He was dealing to kids, for God's sake! When I opened the café door it broke up the party. The youths ran. Murray revved the bike. I didn't need to wonder if he remembered me from last night, it was written on his face. His eyes measured me up, flat and void, as if something behind them had died, then he kicked the prop away and moved off.

There were a lot of new things piling up that I had to talk to Nicholls about; things any average citizen would be queueing up to report, except that some of them were things the average citizen wouldn't have been around to see.

I collected the hybrid and ran it the short distance to Park Square. Grayson & Chubb had offices that put Bentham's into the poverty class. The Georgian square had been slapped with so many preservation orders it almost cost money just to breathe its air, something which in itself gave me a lot of information about Bramfield City and County.

Grayson was busy and Chubb was out of town, but I got to see an associate, one James Bryce who looked to be around thirty and was already balding fast. He didn't

145

really want to pass on information, but my tax inspector's ID card gave me an edge. For the life of me I couldn't see why he was worried anyway, considering that all I came away with was the address of a parent company with a London location. And according to Bryce, he didn't know a damn thing about them.

I was starting to feel like a kid who'd gone out to net tiddlers and ended up landing a pike.

It was half past four and I couldn't think of anything else useful to do around town. I was halfway home when I remembered Charlie and the money I was supposed to give him for Sid. I turned around and headed for a cash point, I'd hate for him to lose faith in me. When I drove into the garage yard there was a slinky two-litre Jaguar taking up a lot of space, and Sid was in the office talking to Charlie. He didn't bother counting the money: like he said, if it was short he'd know where to find me.

I drove home wondering what other line of business he was in apart from supplying picklocks. Whatever it was it paid well.

Palmer's Run is on a gentle slope and I recognised Nicholls' car from near the bottom; I slowed down and took it easy, he couldn't have been waiting for more than nine hours at the most. I parked across the road and walked behind his car and up the steps to the outer door without looking. Some safety conscious soul had remembered to lock it and it took me a couple of seconds to get it open. By then he'd banged his car door hard enough to shatter the paintwork and was pushing hot breath down my ear. He sounded unfriendly again; it came across in the way he steamed: 'Where the hell have you been?'

I asked what seemed a reasonable question of my own. 'Why?' Then I went on upstairs. 'Thanks for putting the boot in with Pete,' I said as I opened the flat door. 'You'll be glad to know he's followed advice on getting me out of the way. I'm down for an unwanted management course in Malvern next week.'

He said, 'Forget about Malvern. Where were you last night?'

I took off my shoes and padded into the kitchen, then I put a new filter in the coffee machine and got it going. After that I answered his question.

'I was home watching the *Rockford Files*.'

'And then what?'

'And then I went to bed. Alone. I gave my teddy away years back.' I changed the subject. 'Did you get the bugs Tom found?'

'Said he found.'

'Found, I was there.'

He said, 'Just how well did you know Mike Perryman?'

I pulled up short at the past tense. *Did* had bad connotations.

'Have you found him?'

'Damn it, Leah, answer the question.'

'We've been there before and the answer hasn't changed – I only knew him through meeting up in court.'

'He never came here?'

'No.'

'And you never visited him at home?'

'No. Look, when I first brought Mike up you said he wasn't your concern.'

'Things change,' he said cryptically.

'Don't they though!'

'An intruder got into Perryman's house last night; why do I think it's no surprise?'

'How would I know?'

'The burglar alarm was triggered.'

'Must have been an amateur,' I said, trying like always to be helpful. 'Which should narrow down the suspects neatly. Look, give me five minutes I need to get out of this suit.'

I trotted off and did a little thinking. There was always a chance some insomniac had been peering out of a window. I took a two-minute shower and decided it was unlikely; if Nicholls knew I'd been in there he wouldn't be on a fishing expedition, no sir, I'd be down at the cop shop making another statement. I pulled on jeans and a yellow sweat shirt and went back to the kitchen.

147

Maybe by now he'd thought of some more interesting questions.

The coffee level had started to go down, but when I scowled a bit he remembered his manners and filled the other mug. Then he tried to slip in a daisy-killer.

'What were you looking for?' he said casually.

'I stayed home, I watched television, drank cocoa and went to bed.'

'What I'd really like to know,' he carried on conversationally, 'is who disturbed who? From the way you took off he wasn't in your friendship book. I bet you scared the shit out of each other.'

That's it about Nicholls, he's nothing if not persistent.

'Going out and finding bona fide criminals must be a real pain,' I said nastily.

The trouble was I had a conscience like lead. Drugs are a dirty business and I'd felt bad enough seeing Murray retrieve a stash from Mike's house, but I'd been feeling a lot worse since I'd watched him deal outside Greasy Joe's. I'd been trying hard to come up with some way to signal what was going down without landing myself on a house-breaking charge. So far, clever ideas were zero.

'You know something, Leah?' he said. 'You're a real pain too. Get your handbag, you're coming with me.' I reached for his mug but he slapped a hand on top. 'Move it. I don't have much time for games.'

I said, 'I hate leaving dirty pots, it's a phobia like wearing clean underwear in case you get knocked down by a bus.' He wasn't impressed. His face had a shutdown look, like a kid waking Christmas morning and finding Santa hadn't been. I walked out into the hall and down the stairs.

He drove without any attempt at small talk and I let him get on with it, these trips to the police station were getting tedious.

Knowing I'm in the wrong always brings out the worst in me. This time I was wrong again. I wondered why we were visiting the hospital.

We turned down past the casualty entrance and by-passed the main car park. Around the back a long, single storey

148

building poked out like an afterthought, its windows small, high up, and glazed with the kind of frosted glass you find in public lavatories. He pushed in through a swing door and marched me down a stump of corridor. The place smelled of formaldehyde and disinfectant, and if he hadn't been hauling me along at a trot I would have hung back. A mortuary was one place I'd hoped never to see.

Tony Murray was lying on a long metal table under one of those reflector lights they have in operating rooms. The top of the table was dropped a bit and his head hung back, his arms stiff at his sides. There was a neat little hole in his forehead and the skin around it was puckered and puffy. The formaldehyde didn't mask the other smells that came up from the table, of blood and death. His lips were peeled back in a stiff smile that showed his teeth. They were surprisingly good teeth, I noted. I could feel my stomach heave. If I threw up so help me, I'd aim at Nicholls.

'Know him?' Nicholls asked harshly.

I nodded. Right then I didn't like the detective sergeant much; a warning of what he was dragging me in there to see wouldn't have gone amiss.

I said, 'You're a real bastard, aren't you?' and swung away. He pulled me back and made me look again.

'Murray wasn't an amateur,' he pointed out roughly. 'He'd been inside, he knew how to look after himself, and he has a hole in his head. Does that tell you anything?'

'It tells me it's wise to know who your friends are, and I don't plan on making his mistake.'

'That's good, that's really good. So what is it makes you think you're invulnerable to bullets?'

'I don't, dammit,' I shouted. 'What do you want me to do, dig a hole and hide?'

'It'd be better than a hole in the head,' he shouted back.

'Thanks,' I said bitterly. 'Thanks a bundle.'

He drove me home and we didn't speak to each other once, which left me with a lot of thinking time. Murray might not have been Mr Nice, but death didn't leave him any potential for change.

149

When Nicholls pulled up on Palmer's Run I offered a truce. 'You're right,' I said, 'I don't need a hole in the head. Come up and I'll put fresh coffee on. It'll be easier to talk that way.'

I could see he read the offer as the indication of a strong desire to bare my soul. That's the trouble with men, you promise a spoonful of sugar and they expect the whole bag.

If he'd thought about it he'd have realised there were degrees of confession, and from where I stood I saw no reason to go to extremes; there were things I had to unload onto Nicholls, and things it would be better for both of us, for him to stay in a state of ignorance about.

I wasted some time playing with the coffee machine while I sorted out priorities. By the time the caffeine had filtered through, so had the patchwork of fact and fiction that had sleepless old me taking an innocent late night ride past Mike's house, and seeing the front room light on. It was a good story, I almost believed it myself.

'It was a real shock to find Murray in there and not Mike,' I admitted. 'There was a piece of floorboard prised up and he had about a kilo of white powder in a plastic bag. It doesn't take a genius to think drugs. He didn't look happy to see me.'

'Putting in or taking out?'

'Taking out, I'm sure about that.'

'Why didn't you tell me before?'

'Wouldn't have helped much, would it? Murray's dead, Mike isn't around, what use is it to know?' I'd said the wrong thing, I knew that as soon as it came out.

He said, 'Try again and this time leave Murray out of the equation, you didn't know he was dead until you saw him in the morgue. You're slipping, Leah. What was the real reason?'

This time the truth couldn't harm me, but that didn't make it more palatable. I'd been putting off saying out loud what I'd already acknowledged in private. Mike was hooked into all this on the wrong side.

Telling it to Nicholls didn't make it sound any better

150

than it had inside my own head. Maybe it's always the same; this wanting people you know, or think you know, to be on the side of the angels. It's one thing setting out to bell the cat, and another to find you're up against renegade mice while you're doing it.

Nicholls digested what I'd told him, and I could see him trying to work out if that was everything. It wasn't, of course. I went right in and told him about the kids at Greasy Joe's. I was glad to get it off my mind. 'I would have told you that anyway,' I said, 'without you camping on my doorstep.'

'But you'd rather have done it without mentioning Perryman.'

I shrugged. 'That's about it.'

He stood up and I waited for him to recite the usual thing. Maybe I should bring some statement forms home then I could have one ready next time the need came. But instead of telling me to get my coat, he said helpfully, 'If you can't sleep tonight read a good book, midnight wanderings aren't healthy.'

He'd surprised me again.

I said carefully, 'So what happens now?'

Nicholls stared at me a while before he decided it was safe to tell me. 'We run another search of Perryman's place and I give hell to whoever botched it the first time,' he said.

'Maybe you're only good at finding things when you're told where to look,' I suggested.

He gave me one of those nice friendly smiles I'd almost forgotten about and stepped out into the hall. I stood in the doorway and admired his butt as he went downstairs.

151

CHAPTER TWENTY-FIVE

I MADE SUPPER, took a bath, and watched Newsnight until it was through, then I pulled the plug and crawled under my duvet. I won't say I was exhausted but it was pretty close and all I wanted was for my mind to quit chasing hares it couldn't catch. I knew there was something running around that needed to be pinned down but I didn't want to spend the entire night worrying about it. One of the hares fell down a hole, and I followed it into dark dreamless oblivion that lasted until I caught up with it just before dawn.

I lay in the dark with my eyes open watching the pattern of light on the ceiling and trying to catch hold of what it was that had woken me. Then I remembered. Just before I'd gone to sleep I'd been wondering if Murray had collected the bullet in his head because of me. I'd walked around the idea and looked at it and finally turned it down as being too much like paranoia, but while I'd been asleep my brain had been busy turning that decision upside down. Tony had been careless, and he'd paid the price.

My foot cramped up and I eased out of bed and padded around until it went off. Let's suppose Mike wasn't only on the edge, let's suppose he was a lot higher up than that, and then let's say he'd had to make a choice between me and Murray. Maybe he'd been having trouble with that long-standing easy friendship we'd shared too; maybe that was why I only got warnings while Tony got a bullet. The idea made me feel cold enough to crawl back under the duvet again. It wasn't that I'd rather have had the bullet, it was feeling a shared guilt in Tony's dying.

I thought some more about Mike's place in things. A Probation Officer's clients are already offenders, and

152

somewhere along the line they've lost sight of the rules by which society governs itself. It wouldn't be hard to hook them into a dependency chain when they were already two nil down in extra time. As many pushers as he needed, always there, on tap.

And the prison system was overloaded, creaking at the seams, drugs were getting in wholesale. Hardly a week went by without a new story breaking in some tabloid or other about lax security. Who better to short-circuit the system than a Probation Officer who could come and go without suspicion, set up a neat network and guarantee supplies. The idea was unpleasant but it wouldn't go away.

I gave up on the idea of getting any more sleep, the light was already changing from pale grey to mellow peach and I knew when I was beaten. I brushed my teeth, washed my face, pulled on my sweats and went out for a run. There's something about early morning that beats the rest of the day, for one thing the air isn't as hung over with exhaust fumes and you can feel it hitting your lungs like a spritzer.

The time I'd spent sleeping hadn't been long but it had been deep and I felt better for it. I did an easy five-mile run that got me home and under the shower in thirty minutes, and felt pleased. I'd kept up a good pace and I kidded myself my body was back in its old shape.

By the time I'd eaten breakfast I could see connections where before there had only been missing pieces. It took a while, but by the time I was ready to walk into town I'd assembled everything I had into a shaky construction that just might hold up.

Beverley was at her usual place behind Probation's reception desk, and we discussed how nice it was that I'd got over the Kawasaki stunt so fast. Then we talked about how odd it was that Mike hadn't turned up yet, and I worried about how she'd feel if he turned out to be as black as my ideas were painting him. When we were through with the sympathy I asked to see Fraser. The chances of him giving me the kind of information I wanted had to be about as remote as a talking goose, but anything was worth a try.

I trotted up to his office on the first floor and tried out my charm. Charm isn't something I feel compelled to use very often, I tend to work on a what you see is what you get principle, but things being what they were I overrode my scruples. Fraser is somewhere in his late forties, bony and sandy with some of the native Scot's burr still lingering after thirty years' exile. He's also quaintly old-fashioned where women are concerned, moving chairs and opening doors as if we'd all been born without arms. Most times I resent that, it's all part of the male power complex, but Fraser was so darned nice it was hard to get ratty about it.

We went through the usual pleasantries about health and weather and then I got down to what I wanted. He looked as if I'd asked him to break into a vault.

I said mildly, 'It isn't exactly a state secret, I'm not asking for names, just numbers.'

'It isn't the sort of information we're supposed to give out,' he protested. 'Clients expect confidentiality. What if I asked how many tax fiddlers you had?'

'I'd tell you. I wouldn't name names but the numbers wouldn't hurt.'

'Perhaps if I knew why you wanted to know it'd be a help. I mean, I don't see what knowing how many of Mike's clients are junkies would have to do with HM Taxes. Forgive me if I'm being a little obtuse.'

'It's a bit of personal research I'm doing,' I said. 'Nothing to do with taxes. Call it a sociological study on the incidence of drug taking in ex-prisoners. I'm thinking about doing an MA.' I hated lying to him but the truth would have been worse.

'Ah, I see, well I suppose that puts a different slant on things if it's to do with academia, it's something I'd have a shot at doing myself if I had the time. But why must it be Mike's clientele, won't my own do just as well? I'm not sure what he'll say when he gets back to work.'

154

'Mike gave me the idea; he said about eighty per cent of his list were users.'

'Never! You must have got it wrong – ten to fifteen maybe, but eighty would be phenomenal.'

'That's why I thought I ought to check back,' I said, 'I'd hate to put the wrong figures in, it would make things look so bad.' That's the thing with a good lie, it's hard to let go. I sat back and acted like intelligent MA material.

He rubbed the bridge of his nose and looked at me. Like I said, he has old-fashioned ideas and I knew he wanted to be nice. After a bit he said, 'You'll not be needing to know right now, will you?'

I worked on looking disappointed. 'I just have three more days to pull it together,' I said, 'then I'm back at work. I was sort of hoping . . .' I let the words trail off to get the right effect. While he was out of the room finding what I'd asked for I thought what a pushover he must be for female clients. I felt like a louse.

When he came back he looked like a man with a lot on his mind, and when I got the figures I wanted I didn't stay around. I had a feeling that as soon as I was gone he was going to start digging around a little himself. Fraser was principal officer, and he'd be wanting to know how come Mike had sixty-five per cent of users when the average was around ten, and how it was *he* hadn't known about it. The guestimate I'd made might have been a little on the high side, but the real number was still enough to worry him.

On the way out I stopped to talk with Beverley again. We talked a little of this and that and then I got back to Mike. Like I told her, when it came to knowing what went on in Probation she had a head start. She looked pleased that I realised that, but when I asked about Mike's women friends she pinked up and shut up. She'd done that once before.

I said, 'He's gay, isn't he?' and got a look of relief that it wasn't something she'd had to tell me.

'It's a real shame,' she mourned. 'I mean – well – you know what I mean.' I agreed that I did and left her to dream impossible dreams.

155

I walked back to Palmer's Run and collected the hybrid, then I took a drive out to the golf club; the swank one where the BMWs had get-togethers. Maybe I'd been wrong in thinking it was too élite for Mike, maybe he'd dabbled in both ends of the market.

I wandered into the bar and parked my bum on one of the genuine-leather stools, they were a deep cherry like the slippers my father used to wear, and well polished with use. The barman had style too, slicked hair and flashy teeth in a young-old face that hadn't travelled many miles but had seen a lot along the way. He was very polite when he told me the bar was for members only, and I liked that.

I told him I was thinking of applying for membership and he didn't blink; that was nice too, the Diplomatic Corps could have used him. There were two examples of female membership in there already, and by comparison I must have looked like I'd make a better caddy.

I said, 'I was hoping a friend of mine might be around somewhere. Perryman, Mike Perryman. Do you know him?'

'Haven't seen him around for – oh – must be a month.'

'That's a shame,' I said. 'Anyone about that he spent time with?'

'Wrong time of day; late afternoon and around one on Sundays are the times he'd be here.'

'Right. I should have checked. What about his friend, er, um,' I snapped my fingers and looked like I was thinking hard 'Denton?' I said. 'Mike talked about him a lot.'

'Funny, I never saw them talking together. Sure he said Denton?'

The women sauntered out, throwing a squinty glance in my direction. Em's poodle wore the same kind of look when she came back from the doggie parlour.

He said, 'The one on the left is Mrs Denton.'

I swivelled round so I could see through the window.

'Expensive looking lady. I thought she'd be older than that.'

He decided I could be trusted and flashed his teeth.

'Second model,' he said confidentially. 'First one ran out of steam. Want a drink?'

'What happened to the members-only rule?'

'There aren't any around.'

'Join me,' I said. 'I'll have a Pils, cold if you've got it.'

He took the tops off two bottles and little whiffs of smoke came out. I paid the bar price and wondered if lunch was included.

'As a prospective member maybe I'd better know your name,' I said brightly. 'I can't go around calling "hey you" every time I want a drink.'

He drank off half his glass and set it below counter level, leaning across the bar. 'Daniel. And since the bar's empty why don't you tell me what you really want and I'll see what I can do?'

'I want to know about Perryman and Denton,' I said.

'Reporter?'

'Tax inspector.'

He liked that. When he'd finished laughing he drank off the rest of his Pils and I bought him another. I hoped the place wouldn't fill up before I got my money's worth.

I said, 'Tell me who Perryman spends time with besides Denton.'

'Those two don't meet up at all, not here anyway. Maybe you've got the wrong Denton.'

'James Aloysius,' I said.

'That's the man, doesn't talk to Perryman though; Perryman's a loner, sits in the corner over there and waits for visitors.'

'What kind of visitors?'

'The younger loaded.'

'Going to hazard any guesses?'

He polished a few glasses and thought about that. Then he downed the second Pils and washed that glass up too.

I said, 'Have another.' He patted his stomach.

'Wind. Whisky helps.'

'Be my guest.'

He poured a double. Now I knew why Rockford had to live in a trailer.

157

He shot the drink down before I could change my mind, and leaned on the bar again.

'I wouldn't want anything I told you to get back to the wrong people.'

'Guide's honour.' I put two fingers up straight and tried to remember if that was Brownies. What the heck, he wouldn't know the difference. 'Sealed lips,' I said. I hoped it wouldn't take another double to soften him up.

He shook his head and eased back.

'The wages here are nothing to write home about but the tips are good,' he said.

What did he take me for?

I took a five-pound note out of my bag and smoothed it down neatly on the bar. 'Suppose I guess and you tell me if I'm wrong, that way you won't have told me anything I don't know already.' I said helpfully.

'You could give it a try,' he said.

'He's selling the kind of stuff that gets to be a habit. Very expensive stuff; in little packets.'

Daniel said, 'I hear his price keeps going up.'

I picked up the fiver before his fingers reached it, and he watched it disappear.

'That's the way it is with market forces,' I told him as I slid off the stool. 'Money's a curse; easy come, easy go. Never can depend on it.'

I'd probably ruined his trust in women, but there were worse ways it could have happened.

CHAPTER TWENTY-SIX

I WENT HOME and got myself a light lunch of omelette and salad, then I put some Vivaldi on nice and low and thought about how well things were coming together. I was starting to enjoy myself again; maybe I should have seen that as a warning.

This time I assembled all my puzzle pieces together on paper, a neat little spider-web of facts and ideas spreading out from Denton's name in the middle. I put my feet up and admired it, it didn't enter my little head that I could be wrong.

All that sitting around exercising nothing but my brain generated a restless feeling, and around three I packed my kit and went down to the health club to work off some excess energy. It seemed a long time since I'd been there and it was like meeting up with an old friend.

Nautilus machines are designed to exercise every muscle, including the ones you don't know you've got and each machine works on a different group. Of course a limb-head with no sense could do himself some real damage if they weren't used properly, which is why everyone using the gym has an exercise programme worked out to suit their own ability. The man responsible for all this is a walking advert for Nautilus' efficacy, and I love the way his muscles move around under his gym kit; a sort of ripple effect you can build fantasies around. His name is Jeff Holt, and quite apart from his looks he's a really nice guy – the kind you'd take home to meet Mother if you weren't too worried she might swoon right off.

He spotted me as soon as I walked in and wanted to know where I'd been for the last three weeks. I told him and he said to cut down on the work-out.

'Take it easy,' he ordered. 'Drop five repeats on each machine and build back up slowly.'

'I feel fine,' I said, 'there's no need.'

'Tell me that on the way out and I might believe it. Five less all round. OK?'

'OK.'

I got changed and shoved my things in a locker, then I trotted into the gym. Bodies rust up a lot faster than cars and that's a fact. It hadn't been that long since the last work-out, but the muscles I'd had then seemed to be on vacation. I felt almost as bad as I did the first time I worked out. I worked my way round grimly until I got to the leg curls; I managed ten, flat out on my stomach on the padded bench with my hamstrings sending out distress signals. The tenth time the roller met my buttocks I decided enough was enough; keeping to normal routine I still had three machines to go, but what the hell, why should I kill myself when so many people wanted to save me the trouble.

I'd sweated so much I had to have lost a half-pound in weight. Maybe that was good considering the unhealthy food I'd been eating lately. I stripped off and stood under the shower until the quivering stopped, then I towelled dry and got into my sweats.

When I trotted out into the reception area Jeff was leaning on the desk. He folded his arms and I watched little ridges move along. *Nice.* He gave me a long slow smile that would have started some quivering of its own if I hadn't learned long ago not to mess with teachers.

'Well?'

'So, you're a know-it-all,' I said and went out the back door. I was glad I'd brought the hybrid, right then home would have been a long way to walk.

The people I share the house with are nothing if not inconsistent; yesterday I'd needed my key to get in, today the front door was standing open. I closed it after me and went on upstairs.

It seemed like I couldn't turn my back for a minute. Someone had left another parcel, wrapped round with

160

string and brown paper like the last one. If this kept on I'd have enough bricks to build an extension.

I opened up and picked up the package; it was heavyish but not brick heavy and I wondered what I'd got this time. Maybe they'd been around the park collecting the kind of stuff I tried to avoid.

I was about to just drop the thing contemptuously in a corner of the hall until I got around to it when a new thought stirred. I stood, half in half out of my home. It looked nice and cosy from where I was; a place to put my feet up and feel safe. I wished I could do that right then. The skin on my scalp felt like skeleton fingers were rubbing it, cold and prickly enough for every hair to stage a walkout. *Shit!*

I held the box very carefully and hustled up what little I knew about bombs. A timer was out, no one knew when I'd be home. Letter bombs went off when they were opened, maybe this would too; or if I dropped it. That last idea worried me; the corner of the hall where I'd almost done just that was very near, I could be lying around in little shreds by now. A fourth possibility crept in; that of someone watching the house, with his finger on a button. I turned around very slowly and started back downstairs with sweat creeping out of my pores.

If it went off I'd never know about it, but somehow the thought wasn't a comfort. I made it downstairs to the hall and along the short leg of corridor to the back door, then I fumbled around with the lock and double bolt and sweated some more. There was a little breeze blowing through the backyard, it felt pleasant and unthreatening. It wasn't a big backyard, the width of the house and about thirty-five feet long, and all it held were dustbins and pot plants that had accumulated over the years to give a half-hearted patio look to the concreted space.

Down at the bottom a snicket gate in the shoulder high stone wall led out onto a narrow access lane. Beyond the lane were the long back gardens of pre-war semis. I wedged the package among the bin bags and other rubbish that almost filled the dustbin, and carried the whole thing

161

down to the farthest corner. Then I made good time to my telephone.

Nicholls, bless his little heart, was still working. I was glad about that, it saved having to explain to some complete stranger why I thought there was a bomb in the backyard. While I was waiting around I went downstairs and knocked on doors like a good neighbour. Only Marcie was home; sometimes I wonder why the ground floor people bother to pay rent. Marcie didn't quibble, she just grabbed her toddler and her coat and handbag, and was out of there, yelling back that if anyone wanted her she'd be at her mother's.

I went back upstairs. Even if the thing went off it couldn't do much damage up there. It was a comforting thought. I wondered how long it took to find a bomb expert. Faintly, in the distance I heard a police siren; maybe that answered the question. Then I heard something else equally familiar and closer to hand, the steady beep-beep of the refuse truck backing down the lane.

Before the council struck the last productivity deal all the bin men would've been home by then, but now that the amount in their pay packet depended on the number of dustbins emptied, they worked their butts off.

By the time I got to the window the bin was jogging briskly to the gate. I stuck out my head and hollered, 'Leave it. Put it down gently and get out of here, there's a bomb in it.' It stopped him in mid-stride and his head slewed round. Then he set off again.

'Pull the other one,' he shouted back.

'Sod it, I'm serious, you bloody nerd; put it down gently and get out.' This time I was talking his language and he got the message. Except for the last bit. I knew he hadn't got that from the way he heaved the bin back at the corner. He didn't wait for it to land to see if I'd been joking, and I didn't wait to see if he made the gate.

After a bit I crawled out from behind the settee and

162

felt silly. I could hear sirens on the street. This was going to be so humiliating. I was worrying about that when Nicholls came in looking anxious. 'God damn it, Leah, what have you been poking into this time?' he snapped.

'Fine!' I snapped back. 'How come it always has to be me? I've been working out at the health club, damn it, what's so wrong with that?'

'So where's the package?'

I walked over to the window and pointed. 'Out there.'

The bin man hadn't been too bothered about keeping things neat. Bin bags had split open and refuse had emptied itself over the yard; it wasn't a pretty sight. It kept Nicholls quiet for a full minute.

I said stiffly, 'It wasn't my fault.'

'It never is,' Nicholls said, and went back downstairs.

It took around an hour to find out there was no bomb. My life hadn't been threatened, except obliquely, but I wasn't feeling good about that.

Standing in the backyard, looking down at what had been in the package, I couldn't believe that earlier that afternoon I'd been listening to Vivaldi and thinking how clever I was. Right then I didn't think I was going to feel that way again for a long time.

I'd managed to push a lot of things I didn't want to think about into the back of my mind, I'd even managed to push Tony Murray there. Now I remembered the hole in his head, and eyes as empty as the dead cat's at my feet, and I knew both were my fault. It had been a nice moggy, with pretty ginger patches splashing black and cream fur, and somebody was going to miss its company.

Red had run, and clotted, and soaked into the newspaper at the bottom of the box. I hoped the knife had been sharp and quick.

This time the thoughtful message hadn't needed any artistic skill, just a few words in thick black marker to point out my culpability. It said, *Your curiosity killed the cat.*

163

Anger, and misery, and guilt all coalesced together in a raging torrent and poured down my face, and just like in an old-fashioned movie, Nicholls pulled out a big white handkerchief for me to catch them in, and gave it to me without saying a word.

Around nine everybody went home. I took a long soak in the bath and then I made some cocoa and a sandwich, and got ready for bed, so bushed I didn't even worry about not sleeping. That was the point Nicholls chose to come back and knock on the door. I was unchuffed, decidedly so, but I pulled on my robe and let him in.

'I hoped you'd all gone home,' I said ungraciously. 'So what is it now?'

He closed the door and wandered into the kitchen. My little mug of cocoa was still on the table and he picked it up and sniffed.

'My mother used to make me cocoa,' he said plaintively.

'Oh, for God's sake!'

I washed out the pan and heated more milk. Anything, I thought, just so he'd go away and let me sleep.

'Right then!' I said, slapping his goodnight drink on the table. 'You've got five minutes to tell me what you want.'

'I came back to check you were all right,' he said, 'that's all. I thought you might be nervous.'

'Nervous? Me? I'm too tired to be nervous. How's the cocoa?'

'The cocoa's good.'

We sat in silence for a while and it finally dawned on me that neither of us was paying much attention to our bedtime drinks. I'd been watching those nice, blue, teddy-bear eyes watching me. It also dawned on me that somewhere along the way I'd stopped feeling quite so bushed, and that certain juices were flowing, so to speak. We stared at each other some more and he got up and came round the table; I couldn't help noticing he dressed to the left, and very definitely so. Oh shit, I

164

thought as my circulation zipped into overdrive, here I go again.

There would still have been time right then to say something flip enough to have the same effect as a cold shower, but I wasn't in a cutting off nose to spite face mood. I got up too, and collided with intent. Close up he smelled interesting, with lots of male pheromones mixed in with faint after-shave and work smells.

He said, 'Leah . . . if you tell me to go I won't give you any hassle.'

'That's nice,' I said and loosened his tie. By the time we got to the bedroom I'd got him half undressed. I hoped he knew what he was about, it had been a long time since I'd shared my bed and I didn't want any anticlimaxes. I needn't have worried, after the first hungry coupling, when we clashed together like gladiators, he was a warm and gentle lover, and I slept contented in his arms until morning.

CHAPTER TWENTY-SEVEN

NICHOLLS COOKED BREAKFAST. Scrambled eggs, plenty of toast, and good coffee. That was nice, the kind of thing I could get used to if it wasn't that I liked living alone. I still had that rosy glow feeling that comes after good sex, and it lasted until I'd waved him goodbye and got down to sorting out my day. Then I didn't feel quite so good.

Tony and the dead cat came back. What right did I have to cause such mayhem? Easy answer. None.

Tax investigator didn't equate with private investigator: people like Rockford got hired to sort out villains, I just got hired to stop money leaking out of HM's coffers. Less romantic but less lethal.

I needed someone to talk to, but not Em, I knew what Em's reaction would be. Round eyes, like the day she caught me up top of the horse chestnut where the best conkers hung out. I got my backside whacked, but the little ape next door never called me sissy again.

I called Tom; he was the nearest thing I had to Rockford. When he offered to come round I thanked him nicely and said if he didn't mind I'd call on him. There were two reasons for that, one was that I wanted to get out of the flat, and the other that I wanted to see where he operated from. I still had notions of a down-at-heel office with a blonde out front, and a bottle of whisky in the bottom drawer.

Sometimes everywhere you look there's a disappointment. Tom's office turned out to be over the Quik-Pass Driving School, and from the street the message T. A. Tinsley, Detective Agency, looked discreet in plain black lettering. On the glass door at the bottom of the access stairs the lettering was even more discreet.

Private Inquiries Undertaken

Debt Collecting

Warrants Served

Missing Persons Traced

I went on up and into a mini reception area with half a dozen padded black plastic chairs, and a two-way intercom box on the wall at the side of the inner door. A thumb tacked card said: PRESS BUTTON AND SPEAK. I always feel a fool talking into machines, but I did it anyway.

Tom stuck out his head and still looked friendly. When he said, 'Come on in,' I trotted past him and looked around. Underfoot he had sage green carpet with a short twist pile, and the three tall filing cabinets were wood faced in mahogany to match the desk. Over by the window he had a low bookcase full of titles like *Jurisprudence, Rules of Evidence* and *Commercial Law*. Three chairs were grouped in front of his desk, low slung enough to stop anyone getting up in a hurry. They carried on the black padded vinyl theme from the waiting room. The chair behind the desk was different, big and easy like Pete's, and I guessed Tom liked putting his feet up too.

'Like it?' he said.

'Nice. I'd add a few pot plants maybe, but apart from that, nice.' I didn't let the disappointment show. Things change; Marlowe would be an old man by now and the mean streets were all pulled down. Well, nearly all. I walked around the desk and tried out the chair; all in all I could quite get to like it. He said:

'Thinking of opening up in competition?'

'Want a partner?'

We grinned at each other and I got up and let him have his chair back. Turning to put my hands on the windowsill I rested my weight on them, watching Bramfield go by. Considering the main road was only twenty yards away the noise was subdued. Whoever had put the double glazing in had done a good job.

167

I said, 'Remember when you told me about the art thefts I thought there was something you held back on? I think I've worked out what.'

'Can't think what you mean.'

'That's what you said last time. Let me run something by you. I read some place that stolen art is easy to sell on the Continent, and drugs are easy to buy. Now let's suppose someone wants the drugs but doesn't want to pay cash. The answer would be to ship over a few paintings, and take payment in narcotics. Only Customs and Excise got wind of it and spoiled things.'

'Worked that out yourself, did you?'

'It wasn't that difficult,' I said modestly. 'Nothing like *The Times* crossword.'

'Leah . . . Look, girl, I promised Ron I'd look after you; don't make it hard. Leave things alone.'

I said, 'Tony Murray's dead and someone killed a nice little cat and left it on my doorstep. I'm sorry, Tom, but I don't think anything I do now can make things much worse.' I turned away from the window. 'I'd really appreciate some good advice.'

'You already got it, from a lot of people. Leave things alone and take a holiday.'

Except I had to live with myself, if I gave way now I'd never have a moment's peace again. I said, 'I think I know who is behind it.'

He digested that. 'Have you told Nicholls?'

'You know Nicholls,' I said brightly. 'He's good at the things he's good at.' Remembering something he was very good at made me feel rosy again. Tom gave me a sharp look, like the feeling showed.

'Always was,' he said on a hard note. 'Too smart for his own boots sometimes.'

Smart? I thought about that. Maybe he was. I didn't know how far he'd really got in sorting things out, and I surely hadn't filled him in on all the thinking I'd been doing either. Mutual lust didn't mean mutual trust.

I said, 'Sometimes I can't see why he hasn't got it all wrapped up, except that the other side always seem one

168

jump ahead. If Regional Crime are really the cream of the crop that's hard to explain.'

'What put that in your head, the one jump ahead idea?'

I shrugged. 'Look, Tom, I'm sorry; I'm wasting your time and you've other things to do.' I began to move to the door, disappointed and knowing I'd no right to feel that way. Tom was doing his brother a favour, he didn't owe me anything.

He sighed, 'Come back and talk about it, for God's sake, I can't stand righteous women.' I went and leaned my bum on the windowsill again, and worried about that one jump ahead business, and how every time I passed on a tit-bit to Bramfield's finest, my troubles seemed to escalate.

'Must be difficult,' Tom said. 'Fancying him one minute and wondering what the hell he's playing at the next.' There was a very funny note in his voice.

I tried to read his face and work out what he was telling me; an idea edged in that I didn't like. Maybe it had been there all the time. I shook my head.

'That's good,' he said, 'you're thinking about it.' I shook my head again, I didn't want to think, I wanted the idea to go away, but Tom kept pushing. 'Things come up that aren't nice, it goes with the territory. If you need to play detective, the first rule of investigative procedure is don't take anything at face value.'

I knew that already; it was a tip I passed on to new trainees. The biggest sharks have the nicest smiles. I said, 'Oh shit, I don't believe what I'm thinking.'

'You're the one who said it. Every time you make a statement . . .'

'Things escalate.'

I'd seen it, recognised it, but needed Tom to make me look at it. The same sequence of cause and effect had been going on right from the beginning; yesterday had just been a continuation. I'd known about Murray and the drugs, I'd told Nicholls, and the next day I'd got a dead cat in thanks.

I wanted to be out of there and Tom knew it; if I'd stayed any longer I'd have cried my little head off on

169

his shoulder, but he still asked what I was going to do next.

I said, 'I don't know, Tom. Honest to God, right now I don't know.'

I came out onto the pavement so sunk inside myself I didn't see the Mercedes until I got hauled in. It was neatly done, and while it wasn't the most graceful way I'd ever got into a car it had to be the fastest.

Leaning against the back seat I rubbed a scraped shin and noted the speedy acceleration. 'Thanks,' I snapped. 'It's nice to be asked so politely.'

Denton said, 'Polite wasn't necessary. It's time we had a talk.'

'About what? Harassment? Need a few pointers?'

Anger tends to make me forget a lot of things, right then it made me forget the tales I'd heard about how nasty Denton could get if he was provoked. Most little girls learn how to pour oil on troubled waters, all I'd ever learned to do was put a match to it.

'You're coming unbalanced,' he said. 'Which is a shame, considering how much damage you could do yourself. Got a call from my accountant yesterday. Seems you're exceeding your official guidelines, Mizz Hunter. Been sniffing around at the solicitor's too.'

'Tell me about it,' I said, 'then explain how Tony Murray got in the morgue with a bullet in his head.'

'I went through that already, when your tame policeman came round. Tony did a bit of fetching and carrying, nothing that could have got him killed. Must have been out free-lancing.'

The Merc had headed south out of Bramfield, and we were cruising on the quiet, scenic road now, on the south side of the lake. The road went nowhere in particular except round the water and back along the other side where the swank houses are. A fringe of ancient wood stretched up a hundred yard slope on our right, with here and there a handy lay-by to admire the scenery from. I got a knot in my stomach thinking how easy it would be to disappear in the soft mossy ground under the heavy

170

branches, but the thought didn't make me prudent, it just made me angry. 'Drugs,' I said. 'Tony was a pusher.' Then I thought maybe I should bite my tongue off.

'Tell me more,' he said softly.

'You know it already.'

'If it was me behind Tony, you wouldn't be having a comfy ride home, you'd be heading for a concrete mixer. That little fracas with the Fiat was a mistake; one of my employees got carried away by enthusiasm and I regret that. He's had his knuckles rapped. The other problems you've been having aren't down to me. I'd like to hear about them.'

A comfy ride home. I eyed Denton. His face didn't look any less tight and cold, but neither did it look more threatening. Too much was happening, I had enough to worry about without Denton adding to the overall confusion.

'You were telling me,' he said. 'About drugs.'

I thought, what the heck, with Tony dead, what more harm could it do him? So I repeated the fumbled deal I'd seen outside Greasy Joe's, and left it at that; with any luck he'd think that was all I knew. And I was about due for a little luck. When I finished, Denton tapped on the glass between us and the musclehead driver, and we speeded up and headed back into town.

When the Mercedes pulled up smoothly outside my place on Palmer's Run, Denton got some manners and reached across to let me out. 'Stick to tax collecting,' he advised, 'it's what you're good at.'

I got out fast before he changed his mind, and thought about how nice it was so many people knew where I lived.

He said, 'Shut the door and be a lady.'

I slammed it. Different bits of my mind were angry about different things. Like the way I'd been hauled into the Mercedes when I should have had my mind on what I was doing. Damn it, I could have ended up as dead as Murray. I tramped upstairs, angry and hurting and sick with myself on a deeper level still. If Nicholls had walked

171

in right then I'd probably have stamped him to death and enjoyed it. Since I couldn't do that I went into the bedroom and stripped the bed right down to the mattress and shoved the whole lot in the washing machine; then I shovelled powder in the slot and hit the boil button.

Around seven Nicholls came knocking on the door. It's a pity minds and bodies don't get together and talk about things, mine were giving off different signals.

I opened the door but I didn't let him in. I didn't know if he believed the splitting headache or not, and right then I didn't care, but it was all he was getting.

He'd brought me yellow roses and I took them through to the kitchen and dropped them in the waste bucket. Then a bit later I sneaked in and rescued them. It wasn't the roses' fault they'd been used as a Judas gift.

Around nine I made a Cuppa-Soup and a cheese and cracker sandwich, and when I'd eaten those I sat in front of the television and pigged on a half-litre of pecan toffee ice-cream. As a comfort food I can't say it did much good.

The thoughts in my head were scuttering around like demented jack-rabbits. Every time I nailed Nicholls down as a bastard I'd remember the feel of him folded around me, and start looking for a way round the truth. There wasn't one, of course. When I was ready to sleep I wrapped myself in the duvet and curled up on the settee, for tonight it felt better that way.

I knew one thing for sure. If anyone thought there was going to be an easy ending they were wrong. Life isn't built that way.

CHAPTER TWENTY-EIGHT

I WAS UP EARLY, to catch a 125 to London that got me into King's Cross just before nine-thirty. When I'd left Bramfield the weather had been iffy, with a pale damp mist that was undecided whether to burn off or settle down to being miserable. By the time I reached London it had made its mind up and there was a steady drizzle that clung like damp spider-webs. I trotted down to the Underground and ran around in circles for a while finding out where I wanted to be. I'm sure Einstein would have found his way along nicely, but I had trouble. Eventually I caught up with a Northern Line train going in the right direction and beat a balding pin-stripe to the last seat. He joined the standers and scowled. Some people are very ungracious about such things.

When I got off at Old Street he was still strap-hanging and looking sour. I smiled at him sweetly as I went by.

The drizzle had now become a steady light rain, heavy enough for an umbrella. I shook out my little fold-up and trotted along the wet pavement. At the corner of Old Street and City Road I turned left and started in reading business plates.

The Companies Act lays down regulations that demand all limited companies to register the names and addresses of shareholders. Bramfield City and County Development Company Ltd had to be so registered or they were running illegally. I could have gone the long way round of course, and tried fishing for information at the company's registered London office, but most solicitors are tight-arses when it comes to discussing clients, and it seemed infinitely simpler to go to the Search Room on City Road and find out for myself; I'm all for avoiding hassle when I can.

It's a fact that in these interesting times everything that can be is computerised or miniaturised to make it inaccessible to Joe Public. I had a real fun time whizzing through microfilm records with print designed to deter anybody who didn't carry a magnifying glass. I hadn't expected it to take that long to come up with Denton's name, but I'm big enough to admit when I'm wrong. City and County turned out to be a wholly owned subsidiary of another company called Ventura Building Projects Ltd. Ho hum.

The search clerk I had to help me bore a strong resemblance to Dame Edna and was bolshie with it. I thought maybe she'd bought the fly-away glasses in her youth and was hanging on to them for sentiment. Her mood was complaining and I was the only target available. I really hate being hectored.

'You do know you're supposed to give prior notification if you need to do a lot of searching around,' she twittered. 'I hope you don't intend to have me running up and down after you all day.'

'I hope not too,' I said truthfully, 'I want to get some shopping in.' I really shouldn't say things like that, Providence seems to take it as a challenge.

Ventura, like City and County, was less than it seemed; a wholly owned subsidiary of a firm called Flint Companies Amalgamation Ltd. I risked a glance at Dame Edna. She was busy reading something at her desk but the pen in her hand wasn't making any moves. I tippi-toed over and took a peek. Mills & Boon fans are everywhere, some days they seem to drop out of the trees. Dame Edna's bosom rose and fell in sympathy as the heroine succumbed to a quick grope in the vineyard.

I kept quiet and hoped she'd turn the page, I wanted to know what happened next. But there we are, between the thought and the deed falls the shadow, and this time it was mine. Dame Edna grabbed for a file to cover up the poor girl's downfall – or not, I would never know. She looked up at me, a little pinker than last time. 'Yes?'

I said, 'I'm really sorry; this whole thing is turning

174

into a dog. Would you believe, this second company is a subsidiary too.' She tsk tsk-ed a bit and got up.

'I don't have time for all this,' she grouched. 'If you're hooked into a ladder of shell companies you could be here all day.'

'I appreciate that,' I said. 'I just saw how busy you were. It's the same with me at Inland Revenue, I'm on the go from morning till night. Would you believe I'm doing this on my own time?' She didn't. The single-word answer was loaded.

'No!'

'As God's my judge,' I said solemnly. 'I'm on official leave and here I am working my butt off, so you can see how I'd really like to get finished up early so I could look around a little.'

'We-ell.' She put a finger on the nose piece of her glasses and gave it a push. 'What company are we looking for?'

'Flint Companies Amalgamation Ltd,' I said.

This time she stayed right with me until it showed up on the screen as another subsidiary. All in all there were a dozen shell companies, with registered offices up and down the country, and I knew I was on to something a lot bigger than I'd expected. To go to that length to hide a holding company showed there were other things to hide too.

Just after mid-day I hit the jackpot and got to the top of the ladder. I'd been wrong about Denton, his name wasn't on Henge Holdings Corporation's list of shareholders. I'd really have to apologise when I got home.

But that didn't mean the name at the top of the list was new to me, I knew it well.

I ran my eyes down the subsidiary companies. I just hated to disturb Dame Edna again.

'It's the last one,' I said kindly. 'I promise.'

It was a very odd feeling to look at the screen and see all the pieces snap finally into place one by one.

Cato Security Services Ltd had fourteen operations around the country. Alphabetically, Titus Security was bottom of the list, but in importance it had to be at the top.

175

Harry must have just about shit himself when he hired Thorne and found out he had a Customs and Excise man on the payroll.

I nudged Denton off centre stage and put Harry there instead.

I suppose the first feeling I had was elation, but after that a kind of sadness set in. It's said that one rotten apple in a barrel will affect the others one by one unless it's rooted out; Harry was out of the barrel now but while he'd been in there, acting like a good and trusted policeman, he'd rubbed up against Nicholls. Of course he must have rubbed up alongside a lot of others too, but I hadn't made cocoa for them.

I walked out slowly, leaving Dame Edna still engrossed in her 'work'. Every now and then the fingers holding her pen would twitch with excitement and I wondered how things were, in the vineyard. I tried to look on the bright side. Love passes a lot of people by, maybe while she was able to read about it there was hope.

Out on City Road the rain had stopped but the grey overcast threatened to start up again any minute. I crossed the road and turned off towards the Barbican. The first time I saw London I was eleven and things have changed for the worse since then, for one thing there are a lot more desperate people about. Filled with guilt I tried not to notice but the closer I got to the centre of town the more they crept into the periphery of my vision: grey shapes in doorways, sagging heaps on damp pavements. If there really was such a place as heaven I'd have a lot of questions to ask when I got there.

I found a place to eat just off Chancery Lane, where the soup was home-made, the French bread crisp and the salad unsagging; I washed it down with an impertinent glass of vinegar disguised as house wine. When I got out a grime-ridden old bag-lady with rimed eyes asked fifty-pence for a cup of tea. The guilt returned and I shook out all the loose change I had in my purse, leaving her rummaging for some place in her clothing without a hole where she could keep it.

176

When the north-bound 125 pulled out of King's Cross just after seven p.m. I had a lot to show for my away-day: a half-dozen picture postcards from the National Gallery, a shirt-blouse from Liberty's that I'd probably insure when I got home, and a little paper carrier bag filled with scrummy chocolate comfort symbols. They were the nice things; the nasties were hidden away in my head.

At W. H. Smith's I'd picked up a Penguin reprint of Highsmith's *Deep Water* that I buried my head in all the way home. It was meant to keep my mind off whatever risky things I might need to do tomorrow, and it seemed an apt choice considering the number of psychopaths I'd met up with lately.

When I got back to Bramfield it was fine but damply chill. I trotted out briskly for home. Just before I got to Dora's I saw Nicholls' car parked outside my place. That was just what I needed: a viper for my bosom. The light was on in Dora's front room and I made a quick right and knocked on her door; it's nice to have friends. We dug the dirt amicably until Nicholls finally got tired of waiting around midnight. By then the comfort symbols were all gone. I said goodnight and went home. There were no parcels outside my door, just another bunch of yellow roses tied up in cellophane. Tucked inside was a little box of Aspirin on which Nicholls had drawn a big question mark.

How nice that he should care.

CHAPTER TWENTY-NINE

SOMETIMES I'M BONE lazy. I couldn't be bothered putting clean sheets on the bed when it was so easy to spend another night rolled in the duvet. I fell asleep right away, and if I had any dreams at all they went on in some place that didn't disturb me. I was glad I'd made a habit out of early rising, it saved all that messing around with alarm clocks.

I can't say I woke up eager to face a new day; the feeling when I padded into the shower was the kind I get when I have a dental visit lined up.

Some of the leaps in logic I'd made would need checking out to stand up in court, but hey! . . . when was I ever wrong? Every place there'd been an art theft Sentinel Security had an offshoot, and not even William Hill's would be dumb enough to take bets on where that led to.

One thing for sure – it hadn't led Thorne any place he wanted to go.

I pulled on a navy sweat shirt and an old pair of jeans that were comfortable enough to sit around in. The running shoes were a precaution, I didn't know how fast I'd have to move. After I'd eaten I made a flask of coffee and trotted out to the hybrid. Things get to be a habit; like the nice, careless way we get into cars and turn on the ignition. I was about to do that when I remembered how disposable I'd probably become. My heart switched to bossa nova and I got out fast.

It's useful to know how cars work, especially when you need to look for bits that shouldn't be there. I spent five minutes crawling around without finding anything wrong, then I got back in and turned the key. If I'd missed something property prices round there were going to plummet.

The engine sang nicely and I drove away and waited for the shaking to stop. Maybe things like this were the reason Marlowe got through so much whisky.

On a side-street across from Titus's chapel I tucked in behind a red Fiesta and settled down to wait. Finding out how many pies Harry had his fingers in had made all the puzzle pieces fit together, but I still needed proof, and unless I was wrong all the way, the place to find it was going to be Watchdog's shipping department. In the meantime I had an intense interest in who his visitors were.

It seems to me that American private eyes have a head start: you wouldn't catch Rockford or Magnum on a stake-out without a neat widow-maker. Most of the time I go along with the anti-gun lobby, but right then it was hard to stay objective, especially when I remembered the way Murray had looked in the morgue.

Ten o'clock came and went and there was nothing much happening apart from security vans coming and going. I started counting bricks in the end terrace house, but that turned out not to be a good idea. I wound down the window to wake myself up again. Around eleven the spiky haired girl tottered out on spiky heels to the corner shop; five minutes later she came back again with something in a white paper bag. I could hardly stand the excitement.

By twelve-thirty I'd been crossing my legs for a half hour, and if I didn't go somewhere soon I'd really mess up my car. If I'd been a man I could have used an old milk bottle; I guess they don't know how lucky they are.

The terrace houses were built back to back and every six houses a passageway led through to the next street; I was glad about that, it saved me having to brave it out and walk right past Harry's office window. I did a fast trot into The Three Tuns.

Around two I was just about stoned out of my mind with boredom. I'd picked up a sandwich in the pub bar, and I was still picking up crumbs of French bread for the hell of having something to do. Across the road the yard was empty of security vans and it was quiet as a graveyard.

I'd about made up my mind to go and talk with Tom

again when Detective Constable Clifford showed up. I hunched down behind the wheel but I needn't have gone to that amount of trouble, he headed into the chapel without looking round. I waited to see what would happen next.

What happened was that twenty minutes later he came out through a side door with Harry, and they were looking very chummy. I gave that some careful thought; I never had liked Clifford. I watched them get into Harry's car and wondered where they were going.

They'd been gone ten minutes when Spiky Hair came out heading for the corner shop again. All those cream buns or whatever were going to ruin her figure. I got out and locked up quietly, thinking how sometimes opportunities drop out of the sky.

Apart from a dog with a drunken sideways trot Chapel Street was empty. I crossed over and eased through Titus's door, ready to come right on out if anyone was around. The magenta walls didn't have any more attraction than they had the first time I saw them, but I guessed there was a point in that. No one doing business there would guess the real size of Harry's operation.

There was no one in the front office and I moved across the tatty carpet to the door Spiky Hair had sent me through last time, easing it open far enough to get a clear view. On the other side of it the corridor was empty. It's a heady feeling to think the Fates are on your side. I gave the stairs a miss, I already knew what was up there, and nobody but an idiot would have a shipping department anywhere but the ground floor or basement. It was a mistake to feel so perky, it should have entered my head that if there are no angels about there must be a fool somewhere. As plans go, the one I had wasn't the brightest I'd ever come up with, but then again I wasn't exactly expert at this kind of thing; all it entailed was playing hide and seek until I found what I knew had to be there.

I was two-thirds along when I heard a door slam and Harry's voice. It sounded pretty near which meant he'd probably used the side door again. Great. Any minute now he'd pop out and be really pleased to see me.

Having only one option to follow saves a lot of decision making.

Against one wall the corridor was lined with odd shaped crates and piles of boxes; there were also less identifiable things lurking under grubby tarpaulins. From the look of them they'd been there a long time. Long enough to have other things lurking there too; hairy things with eight legs. I tried not to think about that, it wasn't a nice thought to hold onto.

There was a musty smell of stale dust and damp plaster overlaid with old oil, and I had an urge to sneeze. Harry's voice came close and passed and I meditated on the few words I'd heard. 'Wrap it up tonight.' It drives me mad catching hold of bits of conversation, and not hearing the end.

I lifted the tarpaulin and squinted both ways, really glad when there was no one about. I couldn't wait to get out from under there. The urge to be a one woman SWAT team had faded, and the thought that occupied my mind most at that point was what a good idea it would be to get out the place. With that in mind I made for the door Harry had used and trotted out into the old schoolyard. I could see the hybrid, it looked a nice little car and I wished I could go and get in. I would have if one of Harry's friends hadn't stopped me. I didn't recognise the flat face, but there was something about his build that put me in mind of fishnet stockings. I got the impression he wanted me to go back inside, and it's hard to refuse a man when he has you by the hair.

He walked me down a flight of basement stairs, and about six from the bottom gave me a vicious push. There wasn't much I could do to save myself except try to roll. Harry said, 'Lenny tends to hold grudges, I've told him it isn't a good thing to do.'

I picked myself up and massaged some new sore spots.

I said, 'I just bet you did.'

I backed up and got the wall behind me. I'd ended up right where I'd wanted to be, but the circumstances were all wrong. There were a lot of packing cases around, some big

181

enough to be coffins; that was a really good thought to have right then. Down at the bottom of the long, stone-walled basement, a metal goods lift stood idle under closed flaps. At one side, a flight of steps went up to an outer door.

From the size of the packing cases, a lot of the stuff they stored and shipped was heavy enough to need the overhead pulley wheel with its dangling hook and chain. I eyed the metal rail that it ran on speculatively.

Harry said, 'I heard you were a bright girl. Shame.'

'Mike told you that, did he? Does he know about Tony, or is that something you've kept to yourself?' His eyes turned sour again and I knew I'd said the wrong thing. I wasn't supposed to know about Mike. I said, 'Don't make any more mistakes, Harry, a lot of people know I'm here. You wouldn't be dumb enough to try keeping me.'

'Don't bank on that,' he said nastily. 'I've got a nice little place just for you, made to measure. Show her, Lenny.'

Lenny shifted from his place at the foot of the stairs and I moved a little as he passed. He skittered sideways, his arms swinging up defensively. I said, 'Why don't you have him wear fishnets all the time, Harry? He looks better with his face covered.'

Lenny didn't like the compliment and started to come back. I got my balance right and waited, I wasn't too confident about disabling him again but it seemed like the only chance I had.

Harry said, 'Leave it and get the crate.' Lenny shot me a vicious look and moved off.

I said, 'Scared I might damage his pride again? You should hire better help.' I came out from the wall. Maybe if I made a lunge he'd drop back and I could make it to the top of the stairs.

He moved out of range. 'I have good back-up,' he said.

I looked at the neat snub-nosed gun resting comfortably in his hand. He held it very professionally; I didn't doubt he could put a bullet through a head with no trouble at all. Over to one side Lenny was shifting a coffin-sized crate from upright to horizontal. Nice. I speculated on how long they could keep me in there before the smell got them down.

I don't know why I have these thoughts, they're not exactly encouraging. I looked at the stairs. A bullet in the back would hurt more than one in the head. I didn't have proof of that but it seemed logical. I turned back to Harry and he nodded.

'Quite right, I wouldn't miss. Try for it.'

'No, thanks. Where are the paintings, Harry? Have they gone, or did Thorne spoil it for you?'

He laughed. 'You had 'em in your loft.'

'I don't mean the rubbish, I mean the paintings you risked breaking into the gallery to get back.' I injected a note of admiration, maybe flattery would take his mind off Lenny and the box. I said, 'Neat scam. Who'd think of looking for a stolen Master under an amateur daub? I suppose "Mr Pickles" would have shipped them to Amsterdam, complete with bona-fide receipt from Bramfield Art Club. It could have worked if Mike hadn't started selling on his own doorstep. I'm surprised you didn't discourage him. And then of course he recognised Thorne. Must have scared the shit out of you to hear you'd got a Customs and Excise man on the payroll.' And it couldn't have done much for Thorne's peace of mind to know Mike could blow his cover. Hearing himself called Robby must have really freaked him out. I said, 'He spent the night before he died with Mike, didn't he, renewing old friendship? And Mike switched the insulin. Not a nice thing to do to a friend.'

Harry shrugged. 'A site accident would have been better. Michael shouldn't have tried to clear up on his own.'

He said 'Michael' affectionately, with a lingering emphasis running over the two syllables like a finger down a cheek, and I knew Beverley had been right. I remembered how broadminded I was about such things. Live and let live. Only with this loving couple it was more die and let die.

I said, 'Thorne picked a bad place to die, didn't he?'

'You should have been working for me,' Harry said, 'it's a shame to waste a good brain collecting taxes.'

183

'Make me an offer.'

'Too late.'

I glanced sideways. Lenny had the crate down flat and his eyes were watching me. He looked expectant, like a cat waiting for a fish-head.

I said, 'You know, it wasn't Mike, or even Thorne, that led me here to you, it was the multi-storey site. I thought Denton's money was behind it, and then I found your name at Companies House. All those shell companies. Such a waste. Where else have you been laundering money?'

He raised the gun and steadied his hand. 'Goodbye, Miss Hunter.'

When Rockford got in a mess like this his police lieutenant friend dropped by to bale him out. I sensed the man with the scythe breathing coldly down my neck, and I didn't want to be dead when I still had things to do.

It's always the same with Nicholls, he really picks his moments. Just before I got to find out about heaven he came in the other door. Harry swung round and moved down the room a bit. I guessed he thought the state I was in, Lenny could handle me if it really came down to it.

Nicholls said, 'Put the gun down, Harry, it's over.'

Of all the dumb, unoriginal things to say. Harry wasn't going to put the gun down, I could see that from the way he stood, squaring up to get Nicholls first before he turned round for me.

I sent up a prayer again – I had to get lucky sometime – and leapt for the hook and chain. The weight of me started it rolling and I curled up my legs and smacked Harry in the back. He was a big man and he hit the concrete floor hard; I let go the hook and used him for a soft landing. Then I got the gun just in case he wasn't as winded as I thought.

'How come you haven't got one of these, you could have got killed,' I yelled at Nicholls. 'I thought policemen were supposed to be bright.'

'Well, isn't that wonderful?' he yelled back. 'I suppose you'd rather I'd waited around so you could get a little ventilation yourself.'

It felt so good to be friends again.

184

CHAPTER THIRTY

BRAMFIELD POLICE CELLS were pretty full that night. I wondered how Clifford felt now he was on the wrong side of a spy hole. Maybe if he was lucky he'd have a pair of flies for company.

Nicholls' file was really thick by now and I knew what it was like to have that much paperwork. He hadn't been as dumb as I'd thought, he'd had a surveillance going on from an upstairs room at the corner shop right from the day Thorne died; which was how he'd got there so fast when I was in trouble. I revised my estimate a little, especially when I found out he'd kept Clifford in the dark about it. I hadn't been the only one to think about cause and effect.

I also got a warm kind of glow knowing that while armed officers were busy deploying themselves strategically, he'd busted right in to the rescue. Thomas Magnum couldn't have done it better.

I'd just have to think of some warm, cosy way to make it up to him.

Friday night Nicholls took me out to eat again and I spent a long time deciding what to wear; sometimes such things are difficult. I didn't want to be overdressed for the local fry-up, but then again I didn't want to look too raggy if we ended up somewhere posh. I settled on simple, sexy and short to keep his mind heading in the right direction.

I climbed into his car and arranged myself neatly. He had a smug look about him and I wondered what it was for. I said, 'Let me guess; tonight it's McDonalds.' He squinted sideways and grinned.

'Try again.'

'The Pizza Hut?'

He shook his head and turned into the Silver Dragon

car park. I was glad I hadn't just worn any old thing. The Silver Dragon serves high-class Cantonese food in a high-class setting, with high-class prices to match and guaranteed *no* monosodium glutamate.

We walked in through the Dragon Gate and got bowed to a table. There were more dragons on the red satin chairs and you could tell they got dusted every day.

The smell of cooking made me famished. By and by the table filled up with interesting things. I was ready to start sampling when the Chinaman came, bowing politely. I took my eyes off the food. Nicholls bowed his head a little and the man went away.

I said, 'Nicholls, you're a scurvy louse, you knew who the Chinaman was all the time.'

I hate it when he looks smug.

I fed him a Wan Tun and ran my other hand up his thigh. 'Eat,' I said, 'you're going to need a lot of energy tonight.'

Well, there it is, everything written down neatly and ready to file away, the only thing missing is what happened to Mike Perryman and I suppose I should set that straight. Let's face it, without Mike's nasty trick I never would have got involved.

It's said every villain has a weakness and Mike had been Harry's. Like any thoughtful lover, Harry tried to keep him safe and bought a real nice place to hide away in. It seemed a crying shame to drag Mike away from the little island in the sun, just so he could spend a minimum twenty years locked up. Knowing what happens in gaol to bent law officers I guessed there'd be times when he envied the man I'd known as Thorne.

That was tough!